A Hood Love in Atlanta Part 2: Unfinished Business

MZ. Demeanor

Dedication

This book is dedicated to the young lovers. The ones that were told they would never amount to anything or make it against the world together. If Mona and Delano have taught you anything; it's that is a lie. You find somebody you love and hold onto them because the world is full of lost people looking to find what you are so blessed to have.

Table of Contents

"One more word and I am taking you both into custody!" The female officer warned.

Daddy was being held back by two officers and one officer stood in front of mama.

"You ain't taking me no gotdamn where because I ain't did nothing yet! Get up off me!" Daddy asserted pushing the officers slightly. The biggest of the two grabbed his arm, but daddy snatched away from him.

"Jason just give me a chance to explain..." Mama begged as he walked past.

"You ain't got to explain shit to me. You run up in here asking about Delano's daddy and think I'ma be cool about it? Come on baby girl let's see what's going on." He directed me before walking down the long corridor.

Mama stared me down as I followed behind him. She yelled something after me that I couldn't quite make out. All we were able to find out was that they were holding Delano for questioning. The whole time we were inside the police station daddy tapped his foot on the floor nervously, that vein in his head protruding. I prayed nobody said the wrong thing to him because it didn't take much to set him off.

The ride home was uncomfortably silent as daddy sped down the street. I knew he was trying to beat mama to the house.

"I gotta ask you a real serious question baby girl and just think real careful before you answer it."

"Yes sir."

"Did you know about this shit with your mama?"

I thought back to the conversation I had with Leslie a while back. She had told me that she saw mama over at Delano's house they day she came to pick me up. How was I gonna be able to tell daddy that without breaking his heart. I never kept secrets before but this would have to be sealed in the vault. After what just happened I didn't want him to be mad at me too.

"No sir, I promise I didn't know anything." I lied.

He looked at me through slit eyes like he didn't buy it then a small smile formed.

"I knew you would've told me. You wouldn't let your pops go out like that. It seems like you are the only person in this family that is still loyal."

Because I felt guilty for lying to him I found something on the radio to kill any further conversation. When we pulled up to the house Marissa was on the porch talking on the phone but got quiet the moment we stepped out of the car.

"Is your mama here?" Daddy enquired stopping right in front of her.

"No sir. I think mama is still at work."

I blew out a sigh of relief as he walked into the house. The last thing I needed was for them to be out here fighting. Speaking of which I didn't know how to approach this situation with Marissa.

"Why are you looking at me like that?"

"I'm just observing a snake in its natural habit." I replied.

"Tahiti let me call you right back girl."
She disconnected her phone call and stood up towering over me.

"I didn't know what your little issue is but you need to watch your tone boo."

"The only thing I need to watch is my temper which I could lose at any minute now."

"Oh so your boyfriend gets locked up and all of a sudden you tough? Yeah, okay try to convince somebody that didn't grow up with ya scary ass."

"I'm scary? We gonna see who the scary one is when daddy find out you been doin porn! Why you quiet now? You the one that wanted to be a dark-skinned version of pinky. Yeah I hear all about the train you got ran on you. I'ma start callin you Amtrak!"

"I-I-I- don't know where you get your information but you got me fucked up!"

"I can back up everything I say sweetie. You done turned into a little bit of a hood celebrity around here. What stripping wasn't enough for you? Now you gotta be all on the internet too?

Her face dropped just like I knew it would. I was bluffing because as far as I knew Todd hadn't put their tape online. I just wanted to see her reaction. She was every bit as guilty as I thought she was.

"You better hope Delano gets out of this mess you put him in because if not I will make it my business to make sure you go down with him."

I walked in the house slamming the door behind me. I was so tempted to beat her ass but I knew it wouldn't solve anything. I waited up all night for Del to call me and give me any type of news but he never called. When I woke up the next morning everybody else was gone. I went down to make me some breakfast when I heard my phone ringing upstairs. Abandoning my omelet I scrambled up the steps just in time to answer.

"Hello?"

"Hey ma how you feelin?"

"Oh my God are you okay Del?"

"I'm coolin ma don't worry about me. They just now letting me get my lil call and I wanted to call you. They said some shit went down up here."

"Yeah my mama and daddy got into it because she was up there to pick up your daddy."

"Wait, what? This whole situation is messed up. They don't have nothing on me they just think if they keep me here long enough I'm gonna confess to some shit I didn't do."

"Del I am so sorry about all of this."

"No worries, none of this is on you. I just need you to be strong but look the dicks is all in my mouth so I'ma call you later. Keep your phone on you and I love you."

Before I could respond he hung up the phone. Knowing that he was okay soothed me a little bit but I was still aware that this wouldn't go away. The sound of the smoke alarm made me race downstairs to the kitchen. Where there was smoke there always had to be a fire which quickly gave me an idea.

"I had not gotten a moments peace since I got here. Todd's parents were in and out of the room constantly and there was a steady stream of nurses and doctors coming in. Glancing at all of the flowers and cards you would have thought Todd was a real life celebrity. I had been nosey enough to read through a few of them but was pissed off after reading them. His crazy ass ex had come up here and had to be escorted out when she got into it with Mrs. Waters.

My baby's chocolate face looked so ashen and lifeless. If it had not been for the steady moving of his chest I would have surely thought I was looking at a corpse. As muscular as Todd was he seemed to have withered away slightly. All of my first had been with him. He took my virginity and my heart and sadly to say it was while he was still with my sister.

Mona didn't know how to handle him like I did. She was so stiff and stuck up that she couldn't have a few drinks and pop a molly to get herself right. He would get me to feel just like I wanted to and would lay up in it all night. True enough he didn't really treat me right but I knew I could change that. I could tame him if I had enough time. I had the body of a woman as well as the mindset and anything a woman could do I could do harder, faster and longer.

I wish I didn't have to go home because Mona knew a lot and I didn't know where she got her information from. She was not about to let me slide with this. I had always been the black sheep of this family so I feel like she was getting what she deserved. Daddy favored her and although mama took up for me, she didn't really look at me any differently than he did.

I always wondered how I could look so much like him and he could hate me the way he did. I found my answer one day by accident.

"Girl I had to go up to that school and go off on Rissa's teacher. She sent her home with some book about being proud of dark skin. What the hell is that to be proud of? My baby is a doll but I guess she took her skin color from her daddy's side."

Mama's word cut like a stab wound. Now I knew what she really thought of me and it hurt. I had to do a book report at school and I chose a book about dark-skinned girls. I thought it would be a good idea sense I got picked on in school sometimes about being chocolate. If I had known mama would get so mad I would have chosen another book.

When I came home and showed mama the book her immediate reaction was anger so I had lied and said Ms. Thomas picked it. She went up to my school the next day and acted a donkey in front of my whole class. Ms. Thomas never got a word in edgewise. I knew she would hate me when I came back to class tomorrow. Now mama was on the phone talking about me like a dog to one of her friends.

I made my way down the hall to my bedroom but stopped short when something she said caught my attention. I was sure I heard her wrong but curiosity made me tiptoe back down the hallway so I could hear her better.

"Girl Jason is still giving me hell about that and it was years ago. I mean damn the girl looks just like him so who's gonna know any damn way?"

There was a loud outburst of laughter as I trudged to my room. It made sense to me now. Daddy was also so hateful to me because I didn't belong to him. I have the same dark skin, dimples, and pretty hair but that must've been a coincidence or either my daddy was kin to him. All I know is now I see why the hell he hated me so much. I was a reminder of mama cheating on him.

I remember crying myself to sleep that night. I always promised myself that I would do whatever it took to make daddy proud but nothing ever worked. I kept my secret locked inside scared to even tell Mona. I always looked up to her and didn't want her to have any reason to treat me differently.

"Hey sweetie, I am gonna take you home so his daddy can stay with him tonight okay."

I kissed Todd on his forehead and followed Mrs. Waters out of the room.

"I hope you don't take this the wrong way but I like you a lot more than I did your sister. I tried to tell my son that those light-skinned girls were trouble."

I smiled as she squeezed my hand before getting on the elevator. For the first time in my life I had somebody actually see something good in me.

I was getting more and more frustrated. This was the fifth time these suits walked out of this tiny ass room. I guess they thought keeping me in here with no windows, no air, and no access to the outside world would make me crack. I wasn't about to tell them shit. They were fishing but I knew they didn't have nothing because they were using the same tricks that they always used.

Detective Lucas had really tried it when he said that they had a witness. Nobody was in the house but me. I made sure of that before I came in. My lawyer was on her way down here so it was really about to be over. I looked up at the camera in the ceiling giving it a wink just to piss them off. Shortly afterwards the door opened.

"Mr. Dawson it looks like you dodged a bullet for right now." Detective Lucas stated walking in.

"You all had no grounds to bring my client in for any type of questioning. Was he even mirandized? Better yet how long was he here before he was able to make a call? Better yet did you have a valid search warrant to search his vehicle?"

Lauren Capperty was the best lawyer in the city. She was well-hated by the prosecutor because she hadn't lost a case in her 11 years as a defense attorney. She was an old friend of pops but I knew she still didn't come cheap. She tucked her bronze curls behind her ear as she waited for a response from Detective Lucas.

"You are slippin Lucky, really slippin. Mr. Dawson you are free to go. My time is money so unless you want to pay me extra you best to be getting up out of here."

"You ain't gotta tell me twice." I replied standing to my feet. I looked at the detective up and down before walking past him. I watched her hips sway in the form fitting two piece suit. Checking out her Red Bottoms I could tell that she was something serious. She summoned me to follow her to a red jaguar when we got to the parking lot.

"Look here let me tell you how I operate so that we are clear. They don't have shit on you. The search of your house and car was a bust plus the car was not supposed to be searched. If they had found anything in there it would have been what we call fruit of the poisonous tree which is just a legal term for illegally obtained information. However, don't think for a minute that you are off the hook. All I want you to do is keep your nose clean and don't do anything stupid like leave town. They are trying to find a way to bait you. Anyway, here is my card and don't you say nothing to those redneck bastards without giving me a call first."

I didn't get to even ask her a questions because she pulled off before I could take in what all she had just laid on me. I thought about asking pops to take over the club until this blew over but knowing him my club would be turned into some 30's and over bullshit. I had to think real quickly and the best idea I could come up with was to ask Courtney. He was a well-respected young business man and I knew he had what it took not to run my club into the ground. Besides he was my business partner anyway so who better to help me out?

I paced around the parking lot waiting on Mona to pick up. Pops wasn't answering his phone which seemed kind of weird to me since he had been down here earlier. His chick came and got him and he left me stranded. This was just a sign of things to come in my opinion.

"Del you okay?" Mona asked finally answering the phone.

"I'm good ma no worries. I need you to come down here and pick me up though.

"Okay say no more. I am on my way right now. Hold tight.

"Where am I gonna go cause I damn sure ain't about to go back in there."

"Yeah you're right I'm just glad that you're okay."

"I will see you when you get here let me get Cash on the phone."

We disconnected the call and I called Courtney up. He had left me numerous text messages and voicemails so I guess word had gotten around pretty quick about what was going on.

"Aye fam you good? Pops came through and gave me the whole run-down."

I thought it was pretty odd once again thee way pops was handling everything. How did he have time to come up to the club and run my business in but didn't even have the decency to wait on me? I was gonna have to check his ass sooner or later but right now my mind was on my money.

"I am good. As soon as I get a shower I will be down there because we got some serious number crunching to do. This lawyer I got is not about to be cheap."

"Word fam, I will be there waiting on you."

After disconnecting the call I paced around nervously as officers kept going in and out of the vehicle. I was paranoid enough to think that they were all looking for a reason to arrest me. Fifteen minutes later Mona pulled up. I didn't even give her a chance to park good before I jumped in the car.

"Oh Del I was scared to death. I thought they were gonna lock you up and..."

I placed my finger over her lips. "Mona you watch too much TV. I told you they ain't got nothing on me. Give me a kiss."

I snatched her face as she leaned into me and kissed her as deeply as I would if I had been gone a few days instead of a few hours. Her curls were getting tangled in my hands but I didn't care as I traced the inside of her mouth with my tongue. I was on brick and wanted much more than a kiss but it would have to wait.

"Ma let's get out of her so I can take a shower."

"Yeah because I didn't wanna say nothing but you smell a little like cheese balls."

I playfully nudged her, "I bet these would be the best chees balls you ever ate though." Our laughter was broken by my phone ringing. When I saw it was Symphony I started not to answer. I was scoping Mona in my peripheral and she was trying her hardest to crane her neck to see who was calling me. I regretfully answered just so she wouldn't think I was hiding anything.

"Talk I'll listen."

"Hey boo are you okay? Cash told me that they took you down to the police station."

"I am definitely cool. They asked me some questions about the nigga Todd because we was beefing but I don't know nothin about nothin."

"Are you serious? I don't know you all that well but you are not cut like these niggas around here. I recall how you allowed him to run his mouth on the radio and you just played it cool."

"I am not in the business of entertaining peons and the only beef I like better come with a salad and baked potato feel me."

She laughed loudly into the phone, "That's why you are my boo cause you keep me laughing."

Symphony had never called me her boo so it did catch me a little off guard. "What you got goin on?" I enquired trying to change the subject.

"I am getting ready to go to work I just wanted to check on my boo before I went in."

There she go with that boo word again. What is she on right now?

"Oh okay well I'ma let you get to that. I am with my girl and I don't wanna be rude to her.

Symphony sucked her teeth noisily, "Yeah let me hurry up and get off here before she find out that you really want some dark chocolate instead of that white chocolate she got."

"Bye I will hit you later." I replied disconnecting the fall before she could say anything else slick. The last thing I wanted to do was argue with my baby right now.

"So I guess she was real concerned about you huh?"

"What are you talking about ma?"

"Okay you gonna play dumb Del? Forget I said anything."

"Mona do we have to keep going through this? I told you that everything with her is business and we have already fell out about it. Can you please pick something else to be mad at?"

"Like I said forget I said anything," She replied turning up the radio.

I was getting real tired of the fussing and jealousy but it was real strange the way Symphony was talking to me. She had a man for one and for two she had never even so much as looked too hard at me before. In the back of my mind I wondered if she was talking to me in front of somebody. I dismissed the thought when we pulled up to Mona's house.

"Thank you for the ride. I am about to run to the crib and then stop by the club but I will definitely be seeing you tonight." I asserted as I stepped out of the car.

"Don't worry about it, I know you got so much business to handle tonight."

I shook my head at this stubborn ass girl but I had more pressing issues to deal with

"So I see you are in your feelings. I will leave you to that and you call me when you feel like acting like you are 18 instead of 8."

I pulled off leaving her standing there with her mouth open. I loved Mona but I was not about to kiss her ass. The attitude was gonna have to go. I rode home in silence so I could think about what my next move would be. I would be lying if I said I want pressed about the money situation because everything I had was tied into my label and my club not to mention the money I had fronted Cash for his party promotion business. I pulled up to the crib taking the steps two at a time. Before I could turn the knob good the door was yanked open. The sight of Symphony in some a red lace brand matching boy shirts caught me completely by surprise.

"Boy come on in before you cause me to give my neighbors a show."

I stepped inside just enough for her to close the door behind me.

"Why are you acting so stiff? You never seen a half-naked woman getting dressed before?"

"I didn't expect you to answer the door like that I'm sorry."

"Aww is my boo shy? I am not gonna bite you D. Matter of fact give me a hug because I was worried about you."

My mind told me not to go anywhere near here but the brick in my pants said otherwise.

"She stood hugged me standing up on her tiptoes. She had that hardness of an athletic body but her ass was so soft as she stood on her tiptoes to make sure I touched it.

"Damn you smell good," she whispered into my chest.

I slowly pulled back but she wasn't letting go. "Uh Symphony are you okay?"

"Yeah I'm good why?"

"You kinda got a nigga in a death grip ma."

She eased up slightly causing me to pry her hands off of me. I don't know if it was because she thought I was about to get locked up or if it was because her man was gone that she came on so strong.

"I am so sorry, I just thought that I had lost you and I guess I started feeling......never mind. Forgive me okay?"

I nodded my head in agreement as she walked towards her room. She bent over to grab her phone of the floor and the shorts temporarily became a thong getting lost between her volley ball size cheeks. *Damn if I was a dog ass nigga I would be all in that right about now. Mona wouldn't know about it.* I almost let my mind get the better of me when realization kicked in. Mona was already accusing me of Symphony so the last thing I wanted to do was prove her right. Besides I didn't need another woman going crazy over me, especially not right now. I got in the turning the water on to nearly all hot. As the scalding water beat down on my body my mind began to drift....

You keep playing with me like you don't want this." Sitting on a bench built inside of the shower Mona opened her legs revealing a perfectly shaved pink peach making my mouth water. Wearing nothing but a white dress shirt with only one button done she was driving me crazy. "What if somebody comes in here? You cool with somebody walking in here to take a shower and catching us?" She laughed. "You worry too much. Come over here and get this before I take that." She replied pointing to the bulge in my basketball shorts. I licked my lips before stepping out of them. She bit her bottom lip as I approached her throwing my shorts in here direction. She caught them smelling them for a second before throwing them on the shower floor. The fog from the hot water gave her an almost angelic appearance as it cascaded around her. Finally reaching her I stood in front of where she sat. Smiling up at me she took my joint in her hand and rolled it between her fingers. The moistness and softness of her hands put me in the zone immediately as she pulled me into mouth. Immediately my eyes rolled in the back of my head. With one hand gripped firmly around my joint and the other cupping my balls she gradually fed herself all of me until she was doing it with no hands. I tried to stifle a moan but she pulled me all the way out before ingesting me like a sword swallower. My toes curled like a polio patient as she grabbed my ass pushing me further into her mouth. I had to hold onto the wall bars to keep my knees from buckling under me. "Yeah you like that daddy don't you? Oh you can't say nothing?" She asked before sandwiching my joint and jewels in her hands slurping both of them at the same time. "Damn ma you gon do it like that?" She looked up at me winking before gargling my joint like some Listerine. I could feel every muscle in her throat contracting as she began to gag slightly. I grabbed my joint pulling out to keep from choking her but she slapped my hand away. She pulled my join out of her mouth and began smacking it over her face and lips before lightly nibbling on the head. I could feel me volcano wanting to erupt so I grabbed her up effortlessly putting her legs on my shoulder. As the water began to beat down on me I pressed her against the wall prying her legs apart before immersing my face in her essence. She gripped my ponytail trying to pull my face away but it only make me find her pear and make it shine for me. "Oh Del shittt!!!!" She yelled causing my tongue to play hide and seek inside of her honeycomb hideout. The convulsions of her body gradually lowered until I could feel her contracting on my tongue. "Ooh daddy......Del....Shittt!! She swung her legs wildly trying to get out of my grasp but I slurped up every drop of the juices I had worked so hard to produce. When she was able to steady her breathing I lowered her onto me. She placed her arms around my neck sneaking kisses every time I

lifted her up. Flexing her kegels she began to milk me for all I was worth.

Nothing I ever experienced felt as right as this moment. She took control

and began using her leg muscles as leverage to bounce up and down on

me. The suction from her grip was starting to render me useless so I

swung around and took a seat on the bench where she planted her feet on

either side of me vaulting up and down increasing her suction with each

drop. I could feel my joint twitching inside of her knowing that any

moment now I would be in another galaxy...............

"Hmmm you keep on yanking like that and you gonna end of pulling it off."

With my joint in my hand I faced Symphony who had pulled back the shower curtain.

"What the fuck are you doin?" I questioned. I was mad and embarrassed that she caught me jacking off in the shower.

"I actually called your name before I came in here but you were a little uh....preoccupied." She replied looking down at my dick that had slowly lots its erection. "I forgot my hand sanitizer in here can you please reach up there and hand it to me.

I snatched the hand sanitizer handing it to her. "Here do you need anything else?"

"Not at the moment but maybe later." She asserted before snatching the shower curtains closed. After she left the bathroom I couldn't even think about finishing myself off because my mood was ruined. Maybe me staying here wasn't gonna be the best idea after all.

"Mo why are you even trippin off that old hoe? You are killin her burnt, bald-headed ass. "

"Les I know what I heard and she was really bein extra kept calling him boo and shit. Do I sound ridiculous?"

"No you sound childish. Why you keep letting her get the best of you? You supposed to be there for your nigga and you letting another woman stress you out. Delano is a good guy, you ain't learned that yet? He look good and yeah he got a big dick and yeah his head is on fire status but…"

She was interrupted by me throwing a pillow at her. "I get the point Les. I need to just trust him. Any man that would risk their freedom for their girl's shady ass younger sister got to be a good guy."

"That is what I been trying to tell you. Now that we got your whining session out the way tell me how I can get with Courtney Cash."

I wrinkled my nose up. "Ugh why him out of everybody?"

"Hold on now, don't front my boo cause he ain't a light bright. Not every nigga can be albino."

"Albino though? You tried it girl. Naw but for real Cash is real serious about his baby mama. I don't think she give that nigga time to breathe because every time his face is not in hers he has to face time her to let her know that it's real. Del said that she trucks him in every sense of the road. They been messing around since grade school though."

Leslie leaned against the wall poking her lips out. "Why can't I find somebody like Del or Cash? I want somebody good too."

"Girl bye. What happened to Bryan, Jaleel, Carmine, and Fab?"

She rolled her eyes. "Hmm let me make sure I get it right. Bryan took more dick than I do. Jaleel go more kids than child support court. Carmine is broker than the investors from the Enron scam, and Fab just got a R.I.P tattoo on his face."

"Oh okay I see your problem now." I replied trying to stifle a laugh.

"It's not funny Mo. Aye hold on what about your daddy?"

I shot her a look. "Don't play with me like that Leslie."

She raised her hands in defeat. Too soon?"

"You know it's too soon. Speaking of which it sounds like I just heard somebody pull up. We raced to my bedroom window in time to see mama pulling into the garage. I got a sinking feeling in the pit of my stomach because daddy had just stepped out to get us pizza and would be back any moment now. I definitely didn't want her seeing what I knew was sure to be a fight.

"Girl I thought you said they got into it real bad today."

"They did get into it. I guess she gonna just roll up in here like nothing happened though. My mama had no class any other time so why was I even surprised now? At the police station was the first time I ever saw my daddy raise anything other than his voice at mama. He may have pushed her away if she got too close to him but he wanted to beat her ass this morning.

"I don't want to put you through this because I know how arguments trigger your issues with your parents."

Leslie shared with me that the reason her grandparents were raising her was because her parents abandoned her. She said all they ever did was argue while they were together but the one thing they did agree on was that they didn't want her. Her mama and daddy took her over to her grandparents so they could go out for a date night. She was 6 years old so she remembered vividly them both kissing her before they left. She never heard from them since and that was 12 years ago. She said the only memories of her parents was hearing them argue with each other.

The sound of another car pulling up snapped me out of my daydream. Me and Leslie exchanged worried glances as we heard the car door shut.

"Let's see what's about to happen." Leslie suggested tiptoeing to my bedroom door. We crept out into the hallway where we got a birds eyes view of the front door. Daddy walked in carrying two pizza boxes and a bag from Rosa's pizza.

"Mona yall come down here and get this food while it's hot!"
We didn't budge as we counted down mentally knowing that it was about to go down Kevin Hart style.

"Jill what the fuck are you doing here? Where ya nigga at from this morning cause that's where you need to be."

"I am tired and don't feel like going through this with you. I pay bills here just like you do so I am entitled to be here and do whatever I want to do while I am in here."

"Oh is that right? You do what you wanna do cause if so that means the nigga been in my house. You might be a hoe but I put it past you to be that stupid."

"I got your hoe Jason! You not gonna keep on talking to me like that!"

"I will say what I want to say and when I want to say it! You embarrassed the shit out of me this morning coming down there to see about the next nigga when you can't see about the one you married!"

"This is for the birds. I will talk to you once you cool down but you are too turnt up right now to listen to anything I got to say."

"Turnt up? Is that how yall talk to each other cause last time I checked you was 40 damn years old!"

"Like I said I ain't going nowhere so you need to move out of my way so I can go take a bath."

"I hope you can fit in the bird bath bitch cause that's the only place you will be getting into to wash!"

The sound of breaking glass brought me and Leslie rushing down the stairs. Mama was trying to duck as daddy picked up every piece of glass he could find and hurled it at her.

"Daddy please stop!" I yelled scared to come any closer to him.

It was like he had blacked out as he completely ignored me. Mama was behind the recliner trying to shield herself from the glass.

"You are being crazy will you please stop!" I pleaded.

"I am about to take my nosey ass back upstairs."

"Jason can you please just hear me out?"

"I don't wanna hear shit you have to say. Just get your shit and get out!"

As their wedding picture crashed to the floor he exited the living room. Mama looked up at me as she carefully crawled from behind the recliner. Her curls stuck to the sweat beading from her forehead, as she stood to her feet dusting herself off. "I bet you just love this don't you? You always wanted us to be split up anyway. Hell for all I know your little bitch ass boyfriend tipped you off and you told your daddy."

All I could do is stand there in disbelief that she was coming to me with this after I had tried to keep her from getting her ass beat.

"Mama I didn't have nothing to do with this. You got your own self caught up."

"Don't think just because me and Jason fell out that you can get smart with me because I will still slap the shit out of you."

Without thinking I stepped into her face. As long as I could remember I was always scared of mama. For some reason she had something against me that stemmed from childhood. I can remember how mean she used to be to me whenever daddy wasn't around. Once Marissa came along it got a little bit better but she was still not the mother she needed to be. At this moment I was tired of her shit.

"I wasn't trying to be smart mama but if you out your hands on me we gonna be in here scrappin plain and simple. I am tired of you always trying to put your hands on me when something doesn't go your way."

She slit those sneaky green eyes at me. I never saw it coming when she reared back and slapped me so hard I thought my head would spin all the way around my neck.

"You are the cause of all my problems and then you think you bout to stand up in my face being disrespectful!"

I examined the blood from my nose before I jumped up knocking her on her back. She tried kicking me off of her but I straddled her clamping my legs around her waist as I started swinging wildly. I was never a fighter but I didn't miss a lick as I wailed on her thinking about all the times she whooped my ass needlessly when I was growing up.

She pulled my hair but it didn't faze me as I went in on her face, chest and everything else I could grab ahold of.

"Mona are you crazy? Get off of here!" Leslie yelled snatching me off of her.

"Naw let go of me Les! I'm tired of her shit!"

I kicked and swung but Leslie would not let go of me even though I was hitting her.

"The hell goin on in here?" Daddy questioned coming through the back door.

"This little bitch just jumped on me!"

Daddy looked from me to mama. "What did you do?"

"Daddy I swear I...."

"I was talking to her."

Leslie let me go helping mama to her feet. "I just told you that *our* child hit me and you ask me what the fuck I did to *her*?"

"Yeah that's about right. I know how you are. What you need to do is worry about that other one that will have to be buried in a y-shaped casket because she can't keep her legs closed!"

Mama sneered at him. "Maybe the reason why I was on somebody else's dick is because your daughter is always on yours!"

The look on his face turned to a dark scowl. Me and Leslie looked at each other not knowing what to do next as he closed in on her. Her back was pressed completely against the wall with eyes clenched tight preparing for the worst.

"I would break your jaw if you were a man but hell you ain't even a damn woman. I don't know if there is a word for what you are .I should have left your trifling ass a long time ago when you got pregnant with some other man's baby. I stayed here trying to do the family thing while you was still out here giving it up to anybody who would look at you." He leaned down close enough to kiss her. "You have exactly one hour to grab whatever you can. You will take your shit, leave this house, and never step foot on my property again. Think I'm playin with you if you want to and you will regret it. You feel me?"

She swallowed hard before nodding the affirmative. He punched the wall behind her before walking away. She gave me the nastiest look before she disappeared upstairs. This was about to get way worse before it got better.

Chapter 5

Marissa

After seeing Todd the other day I couldn't bring myself to go back up there. All of this was my fault and the blood would really be on my hands if something happened to him. All of this really came back down to Mona. If it wasn't for her I never would've even dealt with Todd to begin with. She hogged up all the love from daddy to the point that he had nothing left for me. I never would have went looking for love in anybody else's arm if I had that father that made me feel like I was beautiful. He always heaped compliments on Mona and she just ate it up. I was the one that shared the same dark skin and dimples that he had but he treated me like a step-child. She had the love that I wanted so I took the love that she wanted. It wasn't hard because Todd was never in love with her to begin with.

He didn't even think enough of her to quit Layla's ass. Mona had an issue with her but she didn't try me. She called my number one time and that's all it took for her to know she had the wrong one. Once I met up with Layla at her apartment with Veronica and her older sister that was the end of our problems. I didn't know what I would do if Todd died on me because even though he did some fucked up stuff I had never met anybody I could totally be myself around. If he pulled through we were leaving here and never looking back because as far as I was concerned my family didn't really matter to me.

Mama thinks her taking up for me is showing love but I see through her too. I have tried to get close to her but she is so busy in some man's face that she doesn't have time for me. I've heard her enough of her conversations enough to know the she is messing around with somebody down here just like she was doing back home. My whole life was hinging on Todd's survival because outside of him anybody that truly cared about me was in Kentucky. All I could do was hope for the best with him and have a back-up plan in case he did decided to leave me in this world by myself.

Crunching these numbers hadn't gone the way I planned. The club had yet to turn a real profit which put me in a tight spot financially. The last thing I wanted to do was go to pops for money. I had yet to hear from him even though I was sure that he knew I was out by now. Ten racks wasn't about to be easy to come by.

"Bruh why don't you take a break from that spreadsheet because you are gonna make yourself crazy."

"Cash what am I gonna do? I gotta get this money up man."

"Bruh I wish I could help you out but my bread is tied up too."

"Not only that but Symphony is on some weird shit like all of a sudden she want a nigga."

Cash sat down on the corner of my desk. "I didn't wanna say nothing but since you mentioned it I been getting a bad feeling from her."

"Now you sound like Mona. Don't tell me you with the shit too."

"You want me to tell you the truth or lie to you? I felt like she was meddling in here the other day."

I closed my laptop focusing on him. "What you mean? Meddling in what?"

"I came in here the other night after you had left and accidentally left the door unlocked. Anyway I went to take a piss and when I came back she was sitting behind your desk. She jumped up when I came in here like I walked in on something."

"Why you wait until now to tell me this? She could've been meddling through anything man." I replied irritated.

"I didn't actually see her doing nothing wrong plus you don't like hearing nothing about her. At first I thought Mona-Lisa was just jealous of her too but now I don't know about ole girl."

This was something I would have to keep in the back of my head because if two people thought something was up with her then there was something they were seeing that I wasn't.

"I guess I gotta keep my eyes on her. "

"Yeah most definitely, plus there are plenty of females in the A that can sing if you have to get rid of her."

I hear you but I'm about to get out of here. I'm tired and I gotta be up early to meet with my lawyer."

"Well do what you gotta do and let me know what happens."

I dapped him up before heading out. I wanted to be around for our second open mic night but my stress level was through the roof right now. As soon as I stepped in the car I called Mona.

"Talk to me I'll listen."

I had to laugh because she sounded just like me. "I see you're still in your feelings about earlier huh?"

"No I'm goo just a lot going on over here right now. My parents just got into and daddy put mama plus me and her got in a fight and…"

"Hold up, you was fighting somebody?"

"I'm just tired of her. I feel bad about it now but she slapped me in my face."

"Damn, you need me to come through?"

"As much as I wanna see you right now it a bad time right now. I am trying to get this house together because this living room is a disaster."

"Oh okay well I guess I will see you tomorrow. Are you going to see my lawyer with me?"

"You know I can't miss school. Just let me know what happens. "

I was a little let down about the way she was rushing me off the phone but didn't want to let it show. "Yeah I'll let you know as soon as I find out something."

After we disconnected the call I felt more conflicted her than I was at first. Not wanting to go home I decided to stop by pop's house. I wanted to know why he hadn't rung my line all day anyway. Turning on the radio rapping along with Rick Ross had me distracted to the point of not noticing the black SUV following me.

All of the lights were out when I pulled up which was strange. I called pop's phone but got no answer. Now I was starting to get worried. I looked both ways before reaching under my seat grabbing my glock. I was never one for carrying a gun on me for real but something wasn't right. I looked around cautiously before exiting the car. I knocked on the front door a little harder than was necessary. I waited what felt like 15 minutes but was probably more like 5 minutes.

"Who is it?"

I was relieved to hear pop's voice from the other side of the door. "It's me pops."

A light came on in the living room as he appeared behind the huge glass oval in the front door.

"Boy I been calling down there all day and they wouldn't tell me shit. You okay?" He questioned grabbing me up into a hug. "The hell you doing with a gun on your hip?"

"Hold on, you mean you didn't know I was out?"

He closed the door behind me. "I think I asked you about that gun on your hip first."

"I pulled up and you had all the lights off. I thought something had happened."

He laughed, "I did that because Jill thought her husband was following her when she drove over here."

"So she's over here now? I enquired in disgust.

"Her husband put her out after all the shit this morning down there at the police station. I told her of he brings his ass over here he will get his issue."

"So you don't feel no type of way about what you doing?"

He scratched his freshly shaved head. I mean if you want me to be honest no. She wasn't happy and we...."

"She is my girlfriend's mother though. You know how weird it's gonna be for me when I come around now?"

"I am sorry about that Del but it is what it is. I been lonely for a long time and now I am 42. I don't have but a few good years left so why you want me to be lonely?"

"It ain't that I want you to be lonely but damn I don't wanna be caught up in the middle of this."

He raised up both hands in defeat. "Let's talk about something else. Have you ate something?"

"No sir I am starving too." I followed him into the kitchen where he started pulling Tupperware containers out of the fridge. Looks like he had been going ham in the kitchen because there was yams, ham, green beans, seven layer salad and red velvet cake on the table. "Pops how am I gonna eat all this?"

"I'ma help you out. Get two plates from the cabinet."

He warmed up the food and we were in a good conversation when I heard the stairs creaking. We both looked up as Jill walked into the kitchen wearing a sheer nightgown that left nothing to the imagination. She closed her robe around her when she saw me.

"Oh hi Delano, I was wondering who Dori was down here talking to."

"Dori is your name now?" I said purposely ignoring her.

Eating a forkful of ham pops looked up at me, "I think she was speaking to you."

"Hi Mrs. Middleton." I mumbled under my breath.

She smiled politely before grabbing a yogurt, kissing pops on the forehead and running back upstairs. I was never going to accept that woman as my stepmother so he could hang that up.

"Del I know you don't understand but you have a woman that you love and I have one too. I......"

"Pops I don't really wanna talk about that. I gotta go to this lawyer in the morning so that woman is the last thing on my mind right now. I gotta figure out how the hell I'm gonna pay her."

He sat his fork down in in his plate. "I been thinking about that all day. I think I might have a solution but I don't really know how you gonna feel about it."

My stomach got tight as I looked into his eyes. He had some shit u his sleeve and I wanted to know what it was. He rubbed his freshly shaved head. "Damn I don't even know how to do this other than to just do it."

He walked over to the refrigerator fumbling for something on the top of it. He pulled back a small slip of paper with a number on it.

"Who is this?"

He sighed, "Son just call the number and everything will be explained to you. I just need you to know that once you do this there's no turning back to the way things used to be. "

Observing the worried expression on his face I took the card from him sticking it in my back pocket.

"Well I need to be turning in because she has to work a double tomorrow and it's getting late."

I could tell he was trying to shake me so I complied. After washing out our plates I hugged him and let myself out. A devastating feeling of dread washed over me as I stepped off of the porch and inside of my car. Call me paranoid but as soon as I closed my door I could have sworn I saw a car pull off from the edge of the yard. The same SUV I saw earlier except this time they were driving without lights. Pulling the number out of my pocket I grabbed my phone. Something told me that this number was connected with whoever the hell was following me around. What had pops got me roped into?

My heart skipped a beat as I rode past the residence one more time. I was so afraid that Delano would follow me and I was not ready for him to meet me, not like this. After struggling with my GPS I finally made my way back downtown to my suite at the Hilton. I looked around carefully before exiting my vehicle to make sure there were no cameras around. This whole thing was a huge risk if I got caught. Pulling my baseball cap over my eyes. I scooped my long locks into a ponytail before slipping my shades over my face. Yeah it made me look silly wearing them at night but I didn't need any of my fans recognizing me. Just as I made it through the lobby doors my phone rang. I didn't recognize the number but something in my heart told me it was him.

Not wanting our conversation to be heard I put it on silent as I boarded the elevator. When it stopped at my floor I dialed the number back before swiping the key card on my suite. I grabbed a bottled water while waiting for an answer.

"Hello."

The sound of his voice was so much more masculine than I imagined it would be at 19. I was so blown away that I didn't know what to say at first.

"You called me back so are you gonna talk or what?" He asked impatiently.

"I don't really know what to say. Hello Delano."

"Yeah you know my name but who is this?"

I took a swig of the water before answering. My name is Constantina Giangula."

"Your name is what?" He began to laugh into the phone which kind of pissed me off.

"I said my name is Constantina and I would thank you not to laugh at it."

"My fault ma but I ain't ever heard any name like that, it don't even sound American."

"That's because it is not Delano."

"Were are you from? What do you want with me then? You sure you got the right person?"

"I am definitely sure that I have the right person. You are not making this easy for me. Are you busy right now?"

"I gotta get up early in the morning and it's late."

"Delano please just give me 10 minutes of your time."

He sighed, "Where are you even at?"

"I am at the Hilton in Downtown Atlanta. Are you familiar with this area?"

"The Hilton, damn that's a nice hotel. You must be holding to be staying there."

I wasn't sure what he meant and hoped I wasn't setting myself up to get robbed. I had not really thought this through.

"Give me about 30 minutes and text me your room number."

"Okay, I will see you soon."

As soon as we disconnected the call I texted him my room number before looking for something harder to drink from my suitcase. I came well-prepared with vodka, tequila, whiskey, and some homemade wine I had sent to me from back home. After popping two anxiety pills I pulled a chair up to the window observing the beautiful lights of Downtown Atlanta as I

waited to meet my son.

This is some bullshit. I walked into the lobby admiring the beauty of the hotel. My hands had begun to sweat making me second guess my decision to leave my gun in the car. I grabbed my phone to call Constantina when a lady from the front desk asked me if I needed help. Looking down at my outfit I could see why she thought I didn't belong in here. I had on my lime green Polo shirt with some green and black joggers and my green K.D's. She didn't answer the phone so I had to go over to the snobby old bitch behind the counter and ask for her help anyway. She was surprised when I gave her the room number. "Are you sure this is the correct number sir?"

"Ma'am this is the number she gave me. Is there a problem? Do we need to get a manager?

"No sir not at all. Please give me one moment. She turned away from me dialing up to the room. My stomach was nervous as hell. I knew that whoever this is couldn't mean me any harm because pops never would have placed me in harm's way. What was bugging me was where the accent came from. The name was strange and the accent was strange. I had never heard anything like it.

"Sir you can go ahead and go up and again I apologize for any inconvenience."

I gave her a sarcastic smile before hopping on the elevator. When I got to my floor I took my time stepping out of the elevator. Damn this place was exclusive with the oil paintings lining the hallway. I found her room and knocked on the door.

"One second please."

She had an even more pleasant voice than the one over the phone and when she answered the door my mouth dropped. She had the iciest winter blue eyes I ever saw in my life. He jet black hair hung over her left shoulder and although she looked like a white woman her olive skin indicated that she was definitely mixed with something. She looked sexy in her hotel robe too.

"Please come in."

I followed her into the huge suite. Her huge bed sat on a raised platform in the middle of the expansive room. The flat screen above the fireplace looked to be at least 60 inches and she had a living room section that sat right near the window.

"Please have a seat Delano."

"I don't really have time for that. You wanna tell me who you are though and why you had a nigga drive all the way over here in the middle of the night?"

"I asked you nicely to have a seat but I will not be so nice if I have to ask you again."

"Something in her eyes let me know that she meant business so I took a seat placing my hands on my knees."

"Do you want something to drink?" She offered opening the mini-fridge."

"I don't drink but thank you."

I could tell she was nervous and she had every reason to be with a man in her room that she knew nothing about. The diamonds in her ears and her wedding band let me know that I was dealing with a major bread winner. Everybody pops knew seemed to be connected to money in some form or fashion except for him.

"I guess I should not prolong the time because I know you have to be awake in a few hours. I just thought this would be easier but as I look at what a handsome man you have become I feel like I have been the worst mother ever."

My hands gripped the armrests on my chair. I must have heard her wrong.

"You wanna run that by me again ma?"

"Delano my name is Constantina Giangula and I am your mother."

I sat back in my chair resting my head against the window as I took this all in. She stood in front of me with tears rimming in her eyes and but all I could feel was hatred brewing behind mines. "So you are the same mother that shipped me here like some freight from UPS and left me on my father's doorstep? Or better yet the same mother that never bothered to make a phone call, send a birthday card, or make me soup when I was sick?"

"I wanted to be there but I am so sorry. There is so much that you do not know or probably have been lied to about."

"The only lie I been told was that you was my mam because my mama, that bitch died to me a long time again. The fuck you bring me down here to tell me this shit for?" I jumped up from my seat and proceeded to the door but she stood in front of it.

"Constantine, Ovaltine or whatever the hell your name is, you need to move out of my way because this visit is over."

"I knew that this would happen. I always knew that Dorian lied to you bit I swear in the virgin mother that I tried to be in your life."

I went to pull her out of the way when the click of a gun instinctively made me raise my hands up. I turned around to see a familiar face leering at me.

"Mr. Ralph what are you doing here?"

"Making you disappear if you don't have a seat and listen to what she has to say. And just so you know, if you ever grab my sister again I will shoot you nephew or not."

Now I was real confused as I took my seat. She walked over to the bed and that's when I saw the bathroom where he had been hiding at. She rummaged around through her Chanel luggage pulling out a large wooden box which she sat on my lip before taking a seat across from me. "Open it please."

I looked up at Mr. Ralph who was standing next to her as he gestured with his head for me to open it. Because he still had his gun pointed at me I didn't waste any time opening it. My jaw clenched as I looked at pictures of me. One by one I picked up different pictures of me. Most of the pictures were taken when I was in Detroit with Uncle Pres and Aunt Phyllis but she had a few from when we moved around.

"I have all of you report card as well. I have a few locks of your hair and.........."

She started to tear up.

"How did you get all this stuff?" I finally managed to ask.

"What mother doesn't have pictures of their children? You have been poisoned by your father's lies so much that you don't know the truth. I made a very bad decision and he never forgave me for it."

"How so Constantina?"

"Hey that's your mother boy."

"She ain't earned that title and watch that boy shit before I really give you a reason to shoot me in this muthafucka."

She looked up at Ralph irritated. "Brother give us a moment to talk please."

He sucked his teeth. "Okay but I will be close by if you need me.

As soon as he walked out of the room I breathed a little easier.

"You gonna make this plain for me because I'm lost. That dude was the one that sold me my club and he' your brother? How did you find me? Why come back after all these years?"

She rubbed her hand across her face. "I know all about the club because I was the one that told him to sell it to you. I have been following you around your whole life and you never even knew it. I met your father in the army and yes we had a small fling. I never expected to become pregnant by him and when I found out I panicked knowing that my family would never accept you. I never wanted to give you up but I also knew that I was not ready to go to the states because I had so many things going for me back home. I had done some acting and it was finally paying off. When I told your father e was very upset because he thought I would marry him. "

"So just like that you dipped on me?"

"I am not sure what that means but when I told Dorian how I felt he became enraged and the next thing I knew he was gone. He had went back to the states leaving me to raise you on my own. Of course my family found out and they wanted to kill him but he had left. My family is very affluent and my father is a strict Catholic so he was not about to let me get an abortion. I got to hold you for a few minutes before you whisked away from me. I never forgave my father for it and he died knowing that. Two years later I left Italy in search of you and never returned."

This was a lot for me to take in as I stared into her eyes. All the things I always practiced to say at this moment had left my head.

"I don't even know what to say right now. This shit is crazy. I mean why would you choose right now to make your presence known to me? "

"Your father always had a way to contact me. There has not been an address that you have lived at that I have not sent a letter asking him to let my son call me. I never got a response so I figured that he never gave you any of the letters. "

"Naw I never got nothing from you. Why would pops hold your letters from me?"

"You have to ask him that. All I know is that he reached out to me and told me of a legal problem you have gotten into and I would like to help."

I stood up stretching my arms. "So you thought you would step in and save the day with your money? I would rather sale my club than take a dime from you. I don't want nothing you have. Now it all makes sense why I got that club so cheap, you was behind that too huh?"

"I wanted you to be able to have a legitimate business so that you would stay out of trouble."

"So I sunk all my money in that place thinking I was on some grown man shit when all along you practically gave it to me? That's why you got this mafia ass nigga in here with a gun on me. It all makes sense now. Whatever rock you been crawling under you should have stayed there because I don't need you or nobody else to take care of me. Everything I learned in life my pops taught me and outside of that I taught myself. I don't give a fuck about you or your money. They will put me up under the penitentiary before I take a gotdamn dime from you!"

She looked wounded as I crossed the floor slamming the door behind me. I didn't even worry about Ralph shooting me because the way I felt inside I probably would have welcomed the pain.

Chapter 9

Marissa

I sat in Todd's house eating breakfast when his father came down the stairs.

"Shouldn't this child be in school?" He questioned sitting at the table across from me.

I rolled my eyes because she had warned me that he would be nasty. I had cut school to ride to the hospital with her but had no idea he was still here.

"She is going to the hospital with us of that is okay with you Mayfield."

"It's not okay with me but you are gonna do what you want to do so I won't argue the point. I just think it's awfully damn funny how our son is in this hospital fighting for his life after going through her and her sister. I know one of yall knows what happened to him and I'm gonna do my own investigation because these police are moving a little bit too slow for me."

I had tried to be quiet but he had given me way too much. I loved Todd and blamed myself completely for what happened but I was not about to keep letting him pop shit to me like I didn't matter when I was the key to even coming close to solving this case.

"Mr. Waters I don't know who you think you are but let me tell you one thing or maybe two. For one I love Todd unlike my sister did and for two I am the one that is willing to work with yall to find out who did this to him. We already know who wanted him dead and I am the one that is going to make sure that he gets caught up. You need to quit treating me like I'm the enemy because I am hurting just like yall are. Todd is my first love and I'm having a hard enough time figuring out what I will do if anything happens to him." For dramatic effect I ran into Mrs. Waters arms as she looked at him disapprovingly. Maybe I should look into acting because I had just put on an Oscar worthy performance even managing to shed a few tears. He grabbed his keys walking out of the house while I enjoyed the rest of my bacon, eggs and cheese grits.

My head was all fucked up as Lauren talked to me. Even though she was giving me important information my mind was still stuck on meeting my mother.

"Are you okay because I have been competing to get your attention all morning?"

I looked up at Lauren who was looking real sexy in her black and white hounds-tooth skirt suit. She was looking over her computer monitor at me with her glasses barely hanging on the tip of her nose.

"Yeah just got a lot on my mind."

"Well I need what you have on your mind not to be more important than what I have on mines. As of this morning Todd Water's is still in critical condition but he is stable. I am not the most religious person but I would urge you to pray that he stays that way. Is there anything you want to tell me about the day he got shot?"

I thought about it for a few seconds, "No not really.

She walked from behind her desk standing directly in front of me. "I know you think that this will all blow over and that I am doing this a favor to your father but trust me when I say I don't owe you or Dorian anything. I am here to do my job and in doing that I need to know all of the details so I can represent you in the best way possible because I don't lose. "

"I don't remember what I was doing that night. What you expect me to sit up here and tell you I shot the nigga because that will never happen. I was probably doing something at the club that night."

She smiled at me seductively. "This is why I love my job. You would be eaten alive on the stand because I never said he got shot at night time."

I couldn't do anything but laugh because I had just incriminated myself.

"Like I said Delano you need to pay close attention to what I am telling you because if you make one false move that boy's daddy will make an example out of you. He has enough money to make it happen but he also is underestimating me like you did. Sit up, get you a cup of coffee and watch me work."

Lauren was a cold piece of work as she walked me through the worst case scenario. She was gonna be worth every dime that I didn't have to pay her. The $1500 retainer fee was a drop in the bucket for what I would end up owing her if we went to trial. As confident as she was in my defense I was even less confident in how I would pay her. It was either my car or my club that would have to go to keep but my freedom was worth more than both of them put together.

"What did she look like?"

Delano looked up at the sky biting down on his lip. I could tell he was trying not to be too emotional but it wasn't working.

"She was beautiful. She has the craziest blue eyes like something I never even seen before. She got the kind of eyes that could look right through a nigga. I got my hair her too."

"So do you think that you can ever give her a chance to get to know you?"

"She had 19 years to get her shit together and meet me. Now I'm in a tough spot and she wanna come in and save the day, nah I'm good."

"But Del...."

"Mona my mind is made up about it. I can't even talk to pops right now. He kept all these secrets from me not realizing they was gonna come out sooner or later. I got so many questions. What if I got brothers and sisters? This is just too much to handle at once. I think once this shit blows over I'm gonna strike out on my own for a minute."

I turned his head to face me.

"So you just gonna up and leave everybody that cares about you?

"Of course I would take you with me."

"I can't just up and leave my daddy like that. He is going through a hard time and no matter what Marissa is still my little sister."

Every time I mentioned her name he balled his face up which was kinda cute but annoying at the same time. "You don't understand how I feel. You know everything about your life. Your family is not a mystery to you Mona. I just met a woman I dreamed about my whole life and now she wants to pick up the pieces. You may not be able to stand your mother right now but at least you know her. My whole damn life has been nothing but questions. I don't even think I'm ready for all the shit I'm about to find out and then to make it so bad it comes at the worst time possible."

Delano sat up placing his hands over his face. He was right that I didn't know what he was feeling but he had it twisted if he thought my family was so perfect. We had more than out share of secrets too. I stood up embracing him as he began to cry softly. Keys jingling in the front door caught my attention. Delano wiped his eyes just as Symphony walked in the door.

"Hey yall. I hope I didn't walk in on nothing." She said smiling."

"Nope we were just in here talking."

"If yall in here talking it must have been pretty heavy cause your eyes are red. Maybe you didn't hear me Mona-Lisa because I spoke to you when I came in. I said hey yall so that meant both of you."

"Hi Symphony." I mumbled with acid in my tone.

"My allergies are bothering me." Delano lied.

I was tempted to ask him why he felt the need to lie to her but thought better of it.

"Let's go get something to eat, that might make you feel better."

He stood up following me to the front door.

"You know you can always talk to me if you need me boo." She declared before we walked out.

This bitch was definitely trying it.

"I'll see you later on at the club. I got something I need you to work on for me."

"Anything for you boo." She replied.

******

"Hey baby girl how you doing?" Daddy asked walking into the kitchen where here I was making dinner.

"I'm good. Are you okay because you been gone an awful lot the last few days."

"I just been working hard, it's not gonna be easy carrying all these bills by myself."

"Daddy I could get a job to help. I got less than a month left of school and..."

"Don't worry about nothing but going to school Mona. If I have to get something smaller then I will do that. Speaking of which have you seen your little sister?"

I didn't want to tell him the truth that I had been avoiding her ass like the plague. I didn't trust her and really had no words for her still.

"I just make sure she gets to school and back every day other than that I don't bother her and she don't bother me. Delano's in the living room watching TV." I said changing the subject.

Daddy walked in the living room greeting him while I finished cooking. As soon as got down three plates Marissa sauntered her stank ass through the back door.

"Hey Mona what you cooked?" She asked taking the lid off my mashed potatoes.

"First of all I don't know where you or your hands been at so put my lid down. Second of all I didn't think you would be home. You ain't eatin with your in-laws tonight?"

"You real funny," she replied putting my lid back on my food. "I see you got three plates is mama home?"

"She is in hell where she belongs but Delano is in the living room. You wanna go say hi?"

The panicked look on her face answered my question. She slowly mad her way into the living room being careful to keep her stay short. When I called them into the kitchen to eat Delano had a scowl on his face that would have made Ice Cube cringe. I made our plates while daddy blessed the food. Marissa stayed here punk ass in her room where she belonged which was fine for all of us. The conversation flowed at the table without mama's usual rude ass comments and Marissa looking like a porn star with everything hanging out. This was the way I wished it could always

be but I had to wait to see how it all played out.

I sat in my room fuming while they feasted downstairs. I called mama to see if she could bring me something to eat but as usual she wasn't answering her phone. Delano was really starting to make me hate him. I wasn't too fond of Mona and daddy either. He acted like everything that she did was right. They was all about to be fucked up when his ass got locked up. Then she would know how it felt to have nothing. With Todd's rapping and my dancing skills we would be the lower budget Jay-z and Beyoncé and that bitch would be sitting there writing him letters while he was getting hi booty played with. The thought amused me enough to write in my diary. Looking out of my window I could see into Todd's empty bedroom.

Plenty of times he caught my strip tease through that window. The first time I acted like I didn't realize my curtains weren't closed but I had purposely left them open. I walked out of the bathroom dropping my towel on the floor. As I walked past the window I glanced out and could see him playing his game so I turned on my radio to get his attention. My song Jupiter Love was playing so I got my slow twerk. As I looked back over my shoulder he had damn near crawled out of his window and wasn't shy about letting me know it. That was when I knew I could have him if I wanted him.

He loved showing me off at the studio because I wasn't all stuck-up like Mona was. She would sing on a few tracks and then she was ready to go. I liked to stay after hours when all of the drinks got made, pills got pulled, and blunts were rolled. Most of the times I was the only girl and that's when all the trouble got started. All his homie's were constantly trying me when he had his back turned. Tay was a dude he went to school with. He was short, skinny, acne-scarred and he was the only nigga I knew still wearing braces but he was almost the most respectful to me. Todd asked him to take me home one night because he said he was gonna be in the studio all night but I knew he was meeting up with Layla. I was mad when I left and determined that I was through with Todd's lying ass.

Tay held the door open for me as we walked out into the rain. Todd had just fronted me in front of his friends because I called him out. I knew he was about to go lay up with that ugly bitch Layla because she had blowing up his phone all night. I was holding his phone while he was in the booth and the nigga was too dumb to put a lock code on it. I had been texting her back the last 45 minutes. He told me he had left her old ass alone but these freaky texts she kept sending him said otherwise. I called for him to come out of the booth in the middle of his song so he was mad. All of a sudden I was a groupie when he just had referred to me as his girl.

"Aye bruh can you take her whiny ass home for me? I don't need no kids in the studio fuckin up my flow."

"For real Todd? I asked you why you got that hoe calling your phone and now I gotta leave?"

Todd looked right past me like I didn't even exist. "Like I said can you take her home I got some gas money for you?"

Todd toke one last pull off of the blunt before passing it to the guy next to him.

"I need to be leaving anyway so yeah I got her."

"Grab your shit and be out then. The fuck you standing there looking there looking stupid for?"

I was so embarrassed that if I had been light-skinned it would have shown all over my face. The real groupies sitting in the lounge observed everything from the booth window and were laughing at me which made it even worse. I stood there with my hands on my hip while he continued to stare me down. The nigga even had the gall to blow smoke directly in my face. Tay was sitting there observing everything and obviously felt sorry for me as he grabbed his Jordan back pack and moved towards the door.

"You ready lil mama?" He asked.

"You ain't gotta ask her if she is ready. I said she was ready so she is ready."

I could tell that Tay wanted to say something but he was outnumbered. He dapped up everybody before leaving out. I grabbed my purse and notepad before walking out behind him.

"Aye bruh she do got a fat ass though." I heard one duded say as I walked past.

I shot him an evil look before walking past the lounge groupies. They made no effort to hide that they were laughing at me as I swished past them. Tay held the door open for me as we walked out in the rain. I didn't even think him because I had an attitude. He held open the door to his canary yellow Regal. He had some nice 28's on it that shined under the street lights but I disregarded all of that as I stepped inside slamming the door behind me. I observed the beautiful chocolate leather interior with his name inscribed in the headrests. Everything about this car was custom including the dear shift with a big D stitched on it.

"I know you upset about that monkey ass nigga in there but don't fuck up my shit cause my whip ain't did nothing to you.

"My bad." I muttered crossing my arms.

"You wanna grab something to eat real quick because my girl want me to grab her some chicken."

I looked at him surprised that he even had a girl. He must have caught my look because he grinned at me.

"You hittin me with that I can't believe you got a girl look. It's cool because I get that often but not every girl, is caught up on looks."

I didn't know what to say because he had read my mind but at least I wasn't the only one that thought it. He turned on the radio to kill the awkward vibe in the car. A song I never heard before began to play. The beat was nice causing me to dance a little in my seat. He noticed I was bopping and turned it up as a guy started singing.

"She gave me a chance when they all turned their backs on me/ Had to do five to ten but she stayed unselfishly/ So that's why I gotta get her what she wants/Yeah that's why shorty gets what she needs/That's why shorty gotta get all my time/ That's why cause she's my everything"

"That's a nice sing but I never heard that before."

He cut his eyes toward me. "You like it for real?"

"Yeah it's a break for the same booty shakin music they always making down here. That has a Drake flow to it.

"It's something I've been working on but those cornball ass niggas back at the studio don't appreciate good music."

"That figures because they are used to the same thing as everybody else."

"Hold that thought," he replied pulling his phone out of his pocket.

"Let me guess you changed your mind right" He shook his laughing while she was talking. "Okay what you want?" He paused as she ran down quite a list. "Aye you gonna have to text that to me cause I ain't trying to get cussed out if I grab the wrong thing. Okay baby after I drop my nigga's girl off I will be grab your food and be on my way to the crib." He glanced over at me as if she had said something so of course I rolled my eyes. "I love you too baby."

After disconnecting the call I couldn't help but feel salty because as many times as I told Todd I loved him he never said it back. I couldn't believe that Tay had admitted that he was with a female this late. I guess his girlfriend wasn't the jealous type. I assumed that he would try to get at me like every other dude I came across but he was actually not paying me any attention.

"Why you looking at me like that?" He questioned.

"I'm just wondering how you even know where I live at."

"You live right next door to Todd don't you?"

"Oh yeah I forgot all about that."

"That's because you was too busy in my conversation with baby mama."

"I may have been meddling a little bit." I admitted laughing. "I'm not used to anybody being so polite. If I asked Todd to bring me something to eat in the middle of the night he is gonna have something smart to say and if I do get it you best believe its gon be cold."

"That's because you like niggas like that so that's your fault. My girl is fro, Detroit like myself so she ain't really on that. Plus I think you know what you were getting yourself into cause didn't he used to mess with your older sister?"

My voice caught in my throat because I didn't really to know what to say.

"I used to see your sister go to the studio with the nigga and he would get her to sing on a few tracks then do some dumb shit to make her mad enough to leave so he could call in the same ratchet type of females you saw in their tonight. I almost got in his ass tonight about the way he came to me but I try to let the nigga keep his lil street cred. He can run all that hood shit on them niggas but I know he is a suburbanite. He is scared for a nigga to even know where lay his head at for real because he is around here claiming Bankhead one day and Mechanicsville the next."

He was telling the truth so I just let him talk since he enjoyed doing it so much. He was not lying about Todd's personality and it was the first time I realized how much of a fool I was for dealing with him. When we got close to home I asked him to let me out a few houses down so I could sneak in. I knew mama was at work but daddy's schedule changed constantly. He parked his car and walked with me to the back of the house. He stayed there while I got my key out and crept through the back door. The last thing I remember him saying was that I should have more respect for myself than to deal with a nigga that had me sneaking in the house. By the time I crept upstairs and was able to check my phone Todd had called me about 6 times and left several texts. I read them and each one was worse than the last as eh questioned how long it took me to get home. He mentioned something about calling Tay's phone too and he didn't answer. Not wanting to deal with his shit I just erased his messages and laid down to snag two hours of sleep before I had to be up for school.

That was the last time I ever saw Tay and the beginning of Todd being real different towards me. He started treating me like a hoe in front of his friends and making me drink more. We was popping pills like candy and it wasn't nothing for me to be loving the crew. All the time I really thought he cared about me deep down inside but now as I looked at this window it made less and less sense to me. Maybe nobody cared about my black ass after all. As I look back on it I think Tay was trying to warn me without being a hater. He treated me with more respect in an hour than anybody ever did my whole life and I had no idea where to even find him.

Dorian for sore eyes with his caramel skin, and deep dimples that mirrored my own. We had created the most handsome son in the world and he absolutely hated me. I had to know what he had been poisoning him with all the years because the truth didn't favor either of us too well.

"So does a little kitty have your tongue or are you going to speak?"

He fumbled with the linen napkin in front of him as I grabbed his hand. "I put myself on the line coming down here so the least you can do is tell me why you lied to him."

He snatched his hand away looking me deeply in my eyes. "I told him the truth as I remember it."

"No you told him the truth as you manufactured it. You know that I was not allowed to be a part of his life. Why did you keep him away from me once you saw how much I wanted to be in his life? Yes I made a mistake and all but I tried to make up for it and yet you treated me like I left him on the doorstep in a basket."

"The only reason I agreed to meet with you is so we can talk money. He needs money that I don't have to get him out of this situation. I know he shot that damn boy and almost killed him......"

I cut him off pressing my finger over his mouth. "Are you really discussing this in a public restaurant? What is wrong with you?"

"I wasn't thinking, sorry. I just been under stress trying to figure out how to make this shit right because I can't lose my son, he is the only thing I got in this world Tina."

I bristled slightly as he called me by my nickname. I never allowed anybody else to call me that because it reminded me of him and the life I could have had with my own child.

"The money has never been an issue. In fact he should have had more than enough money to cover him. What happened to his bank account Dorian?"

He took a sip of water which gave me the answer I needed. "So you spent his money? Does he know that you blew through half a million dollars? That was his money for him to do with what he pleased. I trusted you Dori."

He examined his fingernails before meeting my eyes again. "I had some stuff happen and I used a little bit of it."

"How much is a little bit because according to my sources he has nothing left. You not only lied to him about my involvement in his life but you take his inheritance from my father who on his deathbed regretted making me choose between my family and my son?"

"You may have been around in the shadows but I was the one that did all the hard work Tina. I was the one that had to move him from place to place and deal with him hating always being the new kid. I was the one that had to deal with him not having a real damn family to come home to. The boy practically raised himself. I had to be gone a lot on deployments and had it not been for..." his voice cracked slightly "If it hadn't been for my brother and his wife, my son never would have known what it was like to have two parents."

"Yeah a real tragedy what happened to them." I replied taking a sip of my wine.

He gave me a troubled look as if he had read between the lines.

"They deserve the credit for the real values that Delano learned because when I wasn't there and you never was there, they were there."

"Fair enough but I am here now. I can't fix what I did a million years ago but I can definitely fix him going to prison. My son is not ever going to see the inside of a jail cell even if that means I have to resort to something unsavory to prevent it."

"Something unsavory like what?" He questioned.

"You let me worry about that but in the meantime I'm gonna need specifics about this so-called victim and his family. You get this information back to me as soon as possible so we can get this thing resolved. In the meantime I will be back in New York as my vacation will be up soon."

I drained my glass before throwing a few bills from my purse onto the table.

"Why don't you invite your little girlfriend out for a nice lunch?"

All eyes were on me as I promenaded out of the Rathburn's in my black Christian Dior pantsuit and leopard print Louboutin heels.

I couldn't do anything but stare at the screen on my computer. According to the news this nigga Todd was able to talk now. Of course they didn't go into too much detail about his condition but I knew this shit was about to mean a bad day for me. Lauren hadn't called me yet which I took to be a good sign but this right here had me thrown."

"Hey Del you okay?" Mona asked bringing me food from

"Naw I am a little stressed ma."

"I just heard the news." She replied walking around the desk to look at my screen. "Do you think he will really talk?"

"It's hard to say. I mean on one hand I did try to dead the nigga but on the other hand he ain't really tryin to look like a snitch. If I know this nigga he will try to use this shit to his advantage like he is some tough guy because he took a few shells. I don't know man this could turn out a million different ways."

"Speaking of a million different ways, have you talked to your mother again?"

"Mona you know how I feel about that so please drop it why you're ahead."

"I just think you are not being fair Delano."

"Good thing I don't pay you to think."

"Okay since you are in your feelings I will let that slide for now but you don't need to get mad at me because I'm only stating the obvious. I don't know how you feel Del but I do know at this point in your life you need family. You and your dad are on the outs and you don't really know what happened between them so you could at least hear what the woman has to say."

I opened my food as a knock on the door caught our attention.

"Come in."

Symphony walked in wearing a tube top and blue jean denim shorts. The yellow top against her smooth, dark skin looked good on her and the blue jean shorts fit more like boy shorts. I would be lying if I said I didn't look longer than usual.

"Hey yall. Is it a bad time because you said the other day you wanted me to come down here."

Mona rolled her eyes, grabbing her food to go eat in the bar area. I was getting real tired of the petty shit.

"Did I say something wrong?" Symphony asked innocently.

"Why the hell you come in here dressed for a Luke video? You already know I'm gonna catch hell for this later right?"

She raked her hand through her short curls. "She needs to get over it damn Del. I have a nice body and I work hard to maintain it. I am so sorry that she is too scared to show hers off besides we ain't fuckin...........at least not yet."

"What did you say?"

"Nothing boy, I said nothing. Anyway I am off today so you have me all to yourself."

"Actually Cash is coming down here today with some dude he wants me to hear."

She slammed her notebook down on my desk almost smashing my Styrofoam box."

"Aye watch what you doin, what's wrong with you?"

"I don't really care for your lil friend Cash."

"Why he ever do to you?" I questioned sitting back in my chair.

"He just throws off a weird ass vibe. He always staring at me and just undressing me with his eyes."

"It's not like it's too hard to undress you because you ain't never got no damn clothes on."

She placed her hands on her wide hips obviously not finding me funny. "Like I said I don't like him and don't feel comfortable around him so if he is gon be here I will just come back."

"Well do what you gotta do ma. He been trying to get me to listen to this dude for a while so I'm doing it tonight because tomorrow I got shit to do."

"Well I'm already here now so I guess I can just stay. What you got in the box?" She questioned opening the lid.

"Mona brought me a chicken Panini and some salad from some Italian joint called Figo Pasta."

Without asking she took half of my Panini. "So you just take my food without asking?" I grabbed my box away protectively before she could grab it. We were laughing when Mona walked back in mean-mugging.

"I don't mean to break up yall little lunch date but I forgot my pop."

"She forgot what?" Symphony questioned looking at me crazy.

"I don't believe I was talking to you bit I said I forget what yall like to call down here a soda." She replied snatching it from behind where Symphony sat on the corner of my desk.

"See that's why I sad you need to get you a grown ass woman because she is more than just a little bit petty. I think you need to check her before she rubs me the wrong way."

"Mona means well she just doesn't like to feel disrespected. Let me go in here and eat lunch with her before she kills me." I stood up to leave but Symphony sat there picking at my food that she had stolen. It dawned on me that I had never seen her actually eat meat before. As a matter of fact she even told me that the only reason she bought it was because her dude ate it. As a matter of fact he was supposed to be back from his little business trip by now. A whole lot of shit was starting now to add up with her. It was brought back to my remembrance what Cash said the other day about leaving her in my office. I was about to test out his theory too.

"You stay in here while I got her out here so yall don't scratch each other's eyes out. I will be back in a minute. Grabbing my food and phone I walked out of the office closing the door behind me. Mona was going in in on her phone so I knew she had to be talking to no other than messy ass Leslie.

"Girl here he come right now let me call you back." She disconnected her phone stabbing her fork so hard into her food that it pierced the bottom of the container causing Alfredo sauce to spill onto the table.

"You really that mad ma? The girl works in here with me and that's all it is. I hired her to sing and I assure you that's all she is doing now and will ever do period."

"Del I don't trust her and I damn sure don't like her. She does and says little stuff all the time and I know you be hearing her but trying to play it off. I think you need to come from over her house and go back home."

"Now you are talking nonsense because me and pops definitely ain't seeing eye to eye and you know how I feel about your mother. I would be better off staying back over here before I go over there."

"My opinion is you need to leave before it causes an issue for real for real. I know her type of women and....."

"Of course you know her type of women because look at your mama and your sister. Hell even Leslie is ratchet as fuck but I never told you to stop being around her because she is your friend. You need to trust me because I never gave you a reason not to. If you wanna talk about trust we can rewind back a few months ago when you was all hugged up with my security guard and them you left with your ex."

She hopped up from the table. "Okay so that's how you really feel? My mama, sister, and best friend have nothing to do with you or why you wanna keep taking up for that low-budget Indi Arie! Plus nigga don't get brand new because you finally found out who the fuck your egg hatcher is!"

I dropped my napkin on the table. "Okay so now you wanna get personal right? CI am not about to do this with you and you already know why. I will say some shit that will make you go home and call the suicide hotline so your best bet would be to just stop while you are ahead ma."

"What can you say to me that is gonna hurt my feeling Del? What can you say to me? You are the one looking at a life sentence if this nigga snitches on your dumb ass! I will go on with my life and be successful while you will be sitting inn there paying niggas to braid you up!"

I bit down hard on my lip to keep from calling her a bitch. Not only had she just said some hurtful shit but she also showed me her real hand. She was not in this shit til then end like I had thought. My situation was a fucking joke to her. I was caught off guard because I knew in my heart that she was solid but I guess that couldn't be trusted either.

"So all this comes out all over a woman I care nothing about? A woman that was nice enough to let me stay in here house while I was going through some shit at my own. Maybe I would have been better off talking to her because she has shown more loyalty than you are right now. But beyond all that I need you to leave right now."

"I have been kicked out of better places by more important people." She asserted grabbing her purse.

"Aren't you forgetting something?"

She spun around following my eyes to the puddle of sauce that was beginning to drip on the floor from her container.

"The only thing I am forgetting.......is you."

As she strolled out of the club like some supermodel on a runway I smacked her food off of the table watching it splatter everywhere as it hit the floor. She better be glad I was not like Todd because if I was she would have touched everything in this building. Symphony ran out of the office after hearing the commotion.

"Damn what did yall have a food fight in here?"

"Not right now, I am not in the mood. Can you grab me a rag so I can get this shit up?"

"Let me get this up. I think you need to get out of those dirty clothes. Looking down at my white button down and khaki slacks I agreed that a shower was needed. All I had in my office were workout clothes but they would have to do. I turned on the water in the shower and stripped down looking in the mirror as I took my mane down from my signature single braid. I had been toying with cutting it off but I felt like Samson with my hair and now I knew who Delilah was. It was about time for me to get to the shop and get my ends trimmed at least though. While I was thinking this over the bathroom door opened.

"Can I help you?" I asked Symphony unfazed that she was seeing me naked yet again.

"I was just letting you know I was about to step out for a minute. Did you want me to lock the doors?" She made no attempt to hide that she was looking at my joint which amused me. After the way Mona left I guess I was free to do me now. As good as she looked to me and as easy it would be to get her right now my first mind told me to fall back.

"Yeah Cash got his own set of keys so you can grab the keys out of my top drawer." She was so busy dick-watching that she never heard what I said so I repeated myself.

"Okay. I will be back shortly. But uh I hope you got a license to carry that."

"Carry what?" I questioned knowing fully what she was referring to.

"That lethal weapon between your legs."

"Symphony get your corny ass out of here."

Stepping into the shower all I could do was think about the days to come. If this nigga Todd was able to remember anything about what happened I was in huge trouble. I wasn't worried about Petey, Jay-Dubb, Black and Mark didn't concern me because they already knew what it was if they opened their mouth. The clean-up man Ron had disappeared though. The more I thought about how dumb I had been to fall for this shit the more I wanted to kill Marissa's ass too. In fact the only reason she had been spared was because of Moan-Lisa but now that that situation was about to be a dead issue then maybe Marissa would be too.

Daddy handed me $300.00 dollars.

"What is this for?"

"Your mama sent it for your graduation. She said that she has to work and won't be able to make it."

I swallowed back the lump forming in my throat. Ever since she left I had not seen her and to know that she was skipping my graduation was heartbreaking. On top of everything I had just went off on Delano. Part of it was his fault true enough but another part of it was due to the pressure I was under I t was hard siting in this house seeing my parents fall apart like this. As much as I hated the way she treated me I was used to mama being here and her absence was starting to take a toll on me. I know daddy missed her too and that was the real reason he was taking more hours at work. I looked at every bill that came in here and the mortgage payments were paid up for months in advance.

"I know you are disappointed baby girl but me and Marissa will be there plus all of your family from Louisville is coming down."

I gave daddy a weak smile before heading upstairs. Marissa's door was cracked enough for me to see that she was sitting in front of the window.

"I thought you would be u at the hospital. I heard that Todd was able to talk."

Still staring out the window she acknowledged me. "His mama called me but I am done going up there. For one I am tired of the way his daddy talks to me and for two I been thinking about a lot of stuff."

"Like what?"

She turned to face me. "Mona I did you so wrong. I was always so jealous of you that I allowed myself to really do you bad and you are the only person in this world that ever loved me."

I was floored because I had never knew that she felt this way about me. "Rissa we was so close back home, what happened to that. Remember how we used to stay up all night talking and how you never wanted to sleep in your own bed? We used to go to the movies, out to eat, the mall, we did everything together. When you got down here you was on some other and I don't know where it came from."

"It was easier then because I didn't have nobody looking at me. I was 12 when we moved here and now I'm about to be 16. We started being able to have more money to do stuff and live in a nice area and I guess I felt like I needed to upgrade myself to. I just started doing what I saw everybody else doing. If my friends rocked weave I rocked weave. If they got high I got high. If they got drunk I got drunk. All this was about fitting in because you came down here and stopped being fun. You never wanted to do anything anymore so I thought you were boring Mona. I didn't think about it like you was trying to get ready to go off to school."

"Why didn't you just tell me all this Rissa? We could have talked before it got so out of hand. It's bad enough mama and daddy was always at each other's throat."

"You right but at the time all I could see was you had your little boyfriend and that's all you cared about. You didn't have time for me no more. There were plenty of times I wanted to stop dealing with Todd but my whole mission was to make you feel bad. Daddy never had nothing nice to say to me so when Todd was looking at me and giving me that attention it felt good. Daddy always told you how pretty you looked and always bragged about your grades but nobody ever saw nothing good about me but you and once you left me out I had to find my own ways to be happy. You think I liked being a hoe and dancing for these niggas? I was just doing what I needed to do to make me feel important."

I cried as I listened to my sister pour her heart out. All of this had really been my fault after all. I had fell back on my duties as a big sister and it had her childhood basically. We sat there for hours reminiscing about back home. I called Leslie to cancel our shopping trip to get graduation dressed and took Rissa instead. It actually felt good to go out with my sister again. In the back of my mind I thought about Delano too. We were probably better off not being together if these small things kept separating us. I would miss him but at least I had my sister back.

As soon as school was out I walked outside to meet Mona. Today was my birthday and I had no idea what she had planned. Veronica had been blowing up my phone but I was not trying to see her. I was determined to live all the foolishness behind me. I had even prayed from Todd last night which was something I never did. I guess I just wanted everybody to have a clean slate and move on from this. It was hard trying to think of a way to talk to Delano. I needed to apologize to him and let him know I would do whatever I could to help him out of this situation. I hadn't mentioned it to Mona yet because I didn't know how she would react.

When she pulled up I could barely see inside of the car there were so many balloons.

"Happy birthday Rissa." She hugged me before handing me a car in the shape of the number 16.

"Thank you Mona. I love the balloons." I stuck the card down in my bag as she pulled away from the school.

"Mama had the balloons delivered to the house for you and she invited us to dinner tonight."

I had not seen her in almost two weeks so I was a little excited but nervous at the same time because I knew that mama never did anything without some type of drama being involved.

"She wants to have dinner with both of us?"

"Aye, I am just as surprised as you are. I can't believe I was invited."

"Mona what kind of bag is she about come out of because you know she is up to something."

"I wish I could tell you but I'm lost too. She didn't invite daddy so my guess is she is bringing Delano's daddy."

"Speaking of Delano how is he doing?"

She sucked her teeth. "He is okay I guess."

"Don't tell me yall feel out too."

"It's a long story girl but anyway today is about you so let's focus on that."

I left it alone for the moment but before the night was over I was gonna have to find out what was going on with those two. The first order of business was seeing what mama was up to. We stopped by the house to change clothes for dinner. When I saw daddy on the front porch my first instinct was to walk around to the back. I was in a good mood right now and didn't want to be ruined. I knew he was not above doing that even if it was my birthday.

"Both of my girls riding together. I must be dying because I never thought I would see this again. Happy birthday baby girl."

I had to look around to make sure he was talking to me."

"Have I been that horrible that you can't even accept a happy birthday from me?"

"You been pretty rough I can't lie about that." I answered looking down at my hands.

"I deserve that but I hope you accept my genuine apology. I been doing some thinking and today you turn 16 years old. Out of 16 years I can't remember a time we really just spent some time together like a real family. It was always you and Jill or me and Mona except when yall were real little."

Sensing that we needed to talk Mona finally went inside the house.

"It's okay daddy."

"Naw it really ain't okay. You have become a lady right in front of my eyes and I missed the whole thing being mad about something that couldn't be changed."

I didn't know what he was talking about and not sure I wanted to know. I was uncomfortable sitting here talking to him so I wanted to wrap it up as soon as possible.

"Anyway I gotta work tonight but I wanted to give you your gift before I went in."

I blew a breath of relief glad this was about to be over with. He held the door open for me to walk in the house as he followed behind me. Mona was sitting at the kitchen table smiling at me so I knew they had something planned. Daddy walked in front of me into the kitchen where he opened the back door. My heart started to do that fluttery thing as I followed behind him to find a blue Mustang sitting next to his black Beamer.

"YALL PLAY TOO MUCH!!" I yelled running over to the car snatching the door open. It was about a 2008 but I still loved it. My eyes welled up as I started the ignition with the keys daddy tossed me. I got out of the car hugging his neck before I could run back in the house to grab my purse. This was about to be the best night of my life.

Of course mama was fashionably late to dinner. I had chosen Sushi

Itto just so we could try something different. Even though I knew daddy

had to work I felt slightly bad coming over here without him in the car that

I'm sure he paid for by himself.

"She needs to come on because I told Veronica I would bring the car

over there for her to see."

Mona was busy texting that she didn't pay me any attention. "You think she

got lost Mona?"

"As much as she gets around I'm pretty sure she's not lost."

I chuckled picking up on Mona's shade. I was just about to text mama when

the hostess walked up with her not following far behind. She was

overdressed in a royal blue Calvin Klein skirt suit and gold pumps with

studded heels. She had her hair bone straight with a middle part and

makeup was fleeked for the gods. Was it my birthday or hers?

"Look at my beautiful girls. Give your mother a hug but be careful

because these shoes are going back tomorrow."

Mona gave her a half hug as there was tension still there but they tried to

play it off. When I hugged her she grabbed me tight even rubbing my back.

I was all the way on alert now because something was definitely about to go down.

"Sit, sit I have some news."

Me and Mona exchanged confused looks before sitting down. I did notice the huge rock on her finger as she picked up her menu. *I know this woman is not about to tell me she's getting divorced on my birthday.* She noticed me looking at it. "This is not what you think it is. It's actually just a gift from a friend of mines. Don't worry me and your daddy are gonna work this out."

Mona snapped her menu loudly. I knew she was struggling not to say anything smart.

"Daddy got me a car for my birthday."

She raised her perfectly snatched eyebrows. "Oh really? How nice of him. I can't believe he did something nice for somebody other than Mona-Lisa."

"Don't come for me please this is not the time or the place." Mona replied from behind her menu.

I pleaded with my eyes for mama to let it go.

"I brought you here because I wanted to give you my gift. Besides dinner I wanted to get you something special. She reached into her clutch pulling out a small white Pandora box. I could see Mona slowly lowering

her menu as I opened it to reveal a gold Pandora bracelet full of charms.

"There are 16 charms on there. I had to think really hard to come up

with that many."

I held it out for Mona to get a closer look but her look of jealousy

caused me to pull it back quickly. I put it back in the box to keep from

flaunting it in her face knowing that mama had never bought her anything

so expensive.

"I'll be right back I gotta use the bathroom."

I started to follow her but mama grabbed my hand. "Just let her go. She's

mad because you got something good and she can't stand seeing you have

nothing. Let her take her jealous ass on and cry, it's your day anyway."

They have been going up there questioning him but he isn't exactly in the best condition to speak yet. They have been talking to his friends though and I gotta tell you they have been pretty quiet so far. The only thing I'm worried about is the little girl."

"You mean Marissa?"

Lauren looked through her notes. "Yeah that's the one. I am trying to figure out why they have talked to everybody except for her. His mother mentioned her when they spoke with her and she had been visiting him in the hospital so why they haven't spoke to her is beyond me unless......wait a minute she's a minor. They don't want to talk to her until they are sure they have something on you. Do you have a way to get in touch with this girl? I just need to know where her head is."

"I don't talk to her at all because I have nothing to say to her."

"I understand that but can't you get her sister to talk to her? All I want to do is scared her silent. If I can get her to realize she is in just as much trouble as you are then things will be a lot easier."

I knew that Mona was still mad at me and there was no way that Marissa was going to do anything to help me out. This was the worst possible time for me to fall out with Mona because I was gonna need her to try to get through to Marissa for me. Even if she said no it would have been worth a try. "Me and her ain't really talking to each other right now."

Lauren stood up stretching. "I don't care how you do it but you make up with that girl long enough for us to get this over with."

"I'm not trying to hear that Lauren. You are representing me true enough but you can't tell me how to handle my business. With all due respect you just do your job and I'll do mines."

She walked around standing in front of me. "Speaking of payment I would certainly like to know how you were so broke a few days ago but was able to leave $25,000 on my desk."

I looked up at her sideways. "What are you talking about?"

"So now you have amnesia?" Walking around to her desk she slid out the top drawer dropping a manila envelope in front of me. I picked it up and sure enough there was 25 racks in there. "I don't mind taking money because all of it is green but I do not like accepting money from drug dealers. You made it seem like you would an issue paying me and......."

"Lauren please don't disrespect me like that. I have never sold a drug, smoked a drug, shot up a drug, or surrounded myself by other people that did that type of stuff. I told you that I didn't send this money."

"Well if you didn't then who did because your father already told me he didn't do it."

I headed for the door looking back. "I'm sure he didn't but I have a little bit of an idea who did."

I exited her office before she could ask anything else. Scrolling through my phone I found Constantina's number. She was about to hear from me in a way she never expected. It was bad enough she basically handed me my club but now she was doing too much. I couldn't let her come back in and try to fix what she had missed out on but then again I could just use her since she appeared to have an endless supply of what I needed the most...........money.

I can't lie I was heated about Marissa's birthday. Mama did all that just to get back at me. To top it off I was always the good kid and this bitch got a Mustang for her birthday. I turned the radio all the way up on the way home so I didn't have to talk to her. I couldn't wait to graduate so I could get away from all of them. To make it worse Leslie wasn't answering her phone and I had nothing to say to Delano. When we got home I walked in letting the door slam in her face.

"Damn Mona what you mad at me for?" She questioned following me upstairs.

"Girl ain't nobody mad at you."

I slammed my bedroom door which she opened walking into my room.

"You salty because I got some nice stuff for my birthday? You hated sharing the Camry with me and now you got it to yourself. You can't stand to see me shining. It's always gotta be about you getting what you want. Daddy ain't never got me nothing til today so this was basically about guilt anyway. "

I scoffed at here. "Nobody should feel guiltier than mama."

"I'm not even about to do this with you. You wanna be mad then fuck it but don't be mad at me because I didn't nothing to you."

"As I recall you lied to my boyfriend and got me ex-boyfriend shot so I would say you have done the most!"

"Damn Mona I thought se squashed all that the other day but I see you got hidden feelings. You act like you ain't ever did anything wrong." Rolling my eyes I countered with, "Yeah but I never did anything that would cause somebody to go to the pen. You are conniving as hell just like your trifling ass mama."
Snickering she walked closer. "Last time I checked we had the same parents so you may have a little bit of her in you too."

In hindsight I would have thought about what I said next but I was on ten. "Yeah we may have the same mama you win that, but you may want to ask her who your real daddy is."

"Girl bye. I know you think that he belongs to you but he is my daddy just like he is yours and I look just like his ass so are you mad or nah?"

"I ain't gotta be mad because I know who *both* my parents are. You think I'm lying call mama up and ask her who Ivory Cooke is.

The wounded look that came over her face made me regret what I had just said but it was what it was now. I felt like shit as she walked out of my bedroom but something was strange about her reaction. It was almost like she had known something all along. I started to go in her room after her but I had already done enough damage for the night. A few minutes later I heard the squealing of tires and reached my window just in time to see Marissa backing out the driveway almost swiping my car.

"Aye Cash I think we might have something." I dapped him up we continued to listen to the guy singing in the booth. He had an old timey Sam Cooke vibe mixed with some Anthony Hamilton. Although it had never dawned on me to sign a male r & b singer I knew I wanted this dude. He was never gonna be a sex symbol because dude was ugly as hell but his voice more than made up for everything he lacked physically.

"I told you that dude goes in. He used to mess with some niggas down here but they didn't know what to do with his sound. Matter of fact I think he used to rock with that nigga Todd."

As soon as he said that I wanted the nigga out of my booth.

"I know what you are thinkin bruh and trust me he don't rock with none of them niggas no more. Todd was on that same fuck-boy shit with him. He said something about they got into it over a chick Todd was messing with and he basically stopped fuckin with him. He had the nigga come down here from Detroit and promised him some shit he couldn't deliver on to begin with. "

One thing I had always known about Todd was that he was a poser. He came from a different part of Georgia every time he was interviewed and I remember one time a nigga called him on it in a heated rap battle. I wondered if the girl they fell about was Mona but that was neither here nor there because I like his sound and knew I could do something with him.

"Tell him to come here so we can talk business."

As Cash went into the booth to grab him Symphony came into the office.

"I would have been back but my dude just got back in town and we had to get it in real quick."

"Aye you ain't gotta explain nothing to me ma. Did he say anything about my clothes being over there because I don't want no problems?"

She opened her mouth to answer when Cash walked back in the studio with ole dude. Her mouth dropped open slightly but she tried to play it off.

"Aye bruh you definitely did that. You are definitely what the games been missing. I want you to meet my female r&b singer Symphony. He looked at her squinting before extending his hand which she shook very quickly. Something strange was definitely going on.

"Yall know each other or something?" Cash questioned picking up on the same vibe I noticed.

"You look kind of familiar but anyway my name is Tayvon, nice to meet you Symphony."

"Nice to meet you too Tay, I mean Tayvon. I'm always nick-naming people my bad."

"It's cool I actually go by Tay. No disrespect but did you used to dance somewhere?"

"Oh no definitely not I think you may have me confused with somebody else."

"My fault I didn't mean no disrespect."

"None taken. I am about to go grab me a bottled water. Yall want anything from the bar?"

We all indicated that we were good as she hurriedly exited the office. As soon as the door closed Tayvon dropped his head. "Yall fuckin with that girl? She is trouble."

"What you mean trouble?" I questioned sitting in the corner of my desk.

"Man that nigga Todd I was beefing with used to fuck with her. She used to dance somewhere in Decatur and would always come down to the studio. She used to either have real long hair or rock real long weave but I know that's her. Matter of fact she got a tattoo on her ankle that's music notes. She caused me and him to fall out real tough with her scandalous ass."

"I told you D!"

I wiped my face with my hand. I had basically set myself up for failure. Not only had I been staying with her but I also had evidence in her house at one point. Now I was starting to get paranoid wondering if I had left anything behind the night I shot Todd. The way she acted around Tay let me know she was scared of him recognizing her.

"Cash lock the door real quick so she don't walk back in here."

Cash crossed the floor locking the door as I gestured for them to follow me into the booth. I would be careful what I said since I dint know this nigga but I knew I needed to know what all he knew about her. I was really starting to get vexed about the stripper thing too considering she told me she had been working at the hospital for a year as a medical assistant. Closing the booth door behind us I looked Tay dead in the face. "What's up with Symphony?"

Rubbing his hands together he looked from me to Cash. "First of all the bitches name should be orchestra because she done blew on everybody's instrument."

Both me and Cash had to laugh at that one.

"She used to come to the studio downtown before you and Todd fell out. He used to have this one chick that followed him around like a puppy lighting his blunts, carrying his notebook, sucking him up in booth, just a lil young ass girl that didn't know no better. One night I guess his main chick kept blowing up his phone and he cussed his young chick real bad. Symphony was in there that night with some of her friends and they was laughing about the shit. He asked me to take lil mama home for some gas money so I did because me and my girl was struggling at the time and she was pregnant. Anyway, I guess he felt we was gone too long because he blew up my voicemail on some jealous type shit. I went to see him the next day and the nigga had his peoples jump me. After that the nigga avoided me like the plague and just to be petty he had that bitch Symphony call my crib and tell my girl we was messing around and she was pregnant by me. She fucked around and left me after that. I ain't been able to see my daughter since.

All me and Cash could do was shake our heads as he went on to tell us just how much of a snake we had been dealing with. Apparently Symphony had been known to be a little bit of a hoe too which is why Todd beat her ass. I recalled a few months back when she sat in my office telling me the nigga had a history of hitting women. Little did I know she was speaking from personal experience. After chopping it up for half an hour I glanced at the time realizing we had some artists coming in to do some work in the studio. I took his information and let him know I would be in touch real soon. Symphony was beating the door down when we walked back into the office.

"Damn you out here beating like the police." Cash commented opening the door.

"I forgot my phone in here." She replied nastily. "Yall didn't have to lock me out."

I silently cursed myself wishing I had noticed it earlier. I would have loved to see what she had in there. After dapping Tay up Cash followed him out and it dawned on me I hadn't checked my phone. Grabbing it up I went to my security cam app. As soon as it loaded I fast-forwarded it not noticing anything significant until I came across some interesting footage. Earlier Symphony had went into my desk to get my keys while I was in the shower so that part was cool. However, what was fucked up is that after she grabbed my keys she looked both ways before using my keys to open the bottom drawer where my petty cash was kept. *I guess that women's intuition shit was right. Mona tried to tell me about you Symphony but my dumb ass didn't listen. You just showed me who you were but you have no idea who I am.*

Chapter 20

Marissa

"Mama are you serious?"

She sat there fumbling with her keys trying not to look into my eyes. As
soon as I left the house I called her up. I had to know if there was any truth
to what Mona said and if there was then why nobody ever told me. I would
hear things here and there that sounded sketchy in mam's phone
conversations but nothing had prepared me for this. I looked just like
daddy so I knew in my heart this had to be a lie, at least that's what I kept
telling myself. I had his same chocolate skin, wavy hair and dimples. But
here she was telling me that it was true. Everything I knew about my lie was
a damn lie.

"So on my 16th birthday I find out why daddy always hated me so
much, wow."

"Marissa he never hated you he always hated me for what I did but
after you was here he should have let it go. I always loved you because I
planned for you. Me and your daddy were going to be together but......." He
voice trailed off as I fumbled with my hands not really knowing what to do.
When I told her I wanted to talk to her I expected having to go to Delano's

house where we would have some privacy but here we were sitting on a bench in Piedmont Park looking out of place because we were still wearing the clothes from dinner.

"But what? What was the problem? You could have left. I could have had a father that loved me." I looked on my purse for a tissue to dab my bloodshot eyes that had become puffy from the excess crying I had been doing ever since me and Mona got into it.

"You know how my parents were. They were real adamant about me staying with Jason because we already had Mona."

"So you just let them run your life like that?"

She carefully dabbed at the corners of her eyes. "I tried to make my parents see that I could make it work. They never really like Jason because he didn't have much and in the beginning I loved him. I really believed in him until he settled to take over that damn janitorial company. I always wanted a man that came home wearing a suit and tie every day. I wanted to be the wife that had the big house and nice cars to go in the garage. Ivory just had that business swag to him and I knew that if I married him I would never have to clock in at anybody's job because he didn't want me to work."

"So all of this was about what you wanted mama? What about me? Yall thought I would go through my whole life and never find this out? What if I ever needed blood from one of yall?"

She played with the huge rock on her ring finger. "I was thinking about you. You are the child I wanted. Mona was the one that I never wanted to have. She was the one that wasn't planned and the reason I got trapped with Jason to begin with. If it hadn't been for her I never would have married Jason and it would've been just you, me and Ivory."

This was all too much to take in making me feel like I didn't belong anywhere which is how I felt my whole life.

"The whole reason we even came down here was because I was about to leave Jason. I had reconnected with Ivory and we had met up a couple of times. He had just went through a divorce and I wasn't happy so we had basically made it official that we were getting back together but your daddy found out about it and all of a sudden he was willing to leave Louisville like I had been begging him to do for years."

"How did you end up with Delano's daddy then?"

She threw her hand up. "We met online when I figured out I was gonna be moving here. I needed something to do here because me and Jason ain't been getting it in?"

I wrinkled my nose in disgust.

"Well it's the truth. He acted like he was too disgusted to touch me after me and Ivory had been hooking up. He even tried to make me get an aids test just to humiliate me. What I want to know is why the hell Mona told you this because I know she only got it from her daddy."

Feeling the tears build back up in my eyes I added, "I don't know why she told me either. I would have been better off with thinking daddy hated me than to find out this on my birthday."

Mama hugged me tightly. "I am so sorry you had to find out like this. I am even sorrier that hateful little wench told you like she did but at the same time I am relieved because lying was starting to be too tiresome." Taking a deep breath I looked into mama's beautiful emerald colored eyes. I had never seen her look more sincere than she did at this moment.

"So do you know where he is now?"

My question caught her off guard causing her smile to fade quickly. I was hoping you wouldn't ask that just yet but I know where is."

"Do you think he would want to talk to me?"

The look on her face gave me my answer. He had no intention of ever laying eyes on me. I tried to play it off but the pain that shot through my heart was unbearable. Here was yet another man that didn't want me.

It felt like a million strings were being pulled in my back as I struggled to sit up. For the first time in a while I was in my room by my damn self. As soon as I was able to talk detectives had ben hounding me to tell them my story. I could only recall bits and pieces about that night but I definitely knew who tried to kill me. Now that I think about it Marissa's ass knew what she was doing when she came up with this plan. Yeah I had knocked her ass around a few times but it was only because she was so damn easy. She was nothing like Layla's crazy ass. I f I told her to shut up she got quiet, If I told her to fix me something to eat she did it, If I told her to fuck the whole crew she even did that. Marissa was fun, beautiful and obedient and I loved that about her at first.

Everybody respected me more when I stopped bring Layla around because I finally had a girl that would listen to what I said and hung on to my heavy word. I probably should feel bad about the way I did Mona but I didn't. I wasn't stupid about what was going on in my own house. I knew my daddy didn't respect my mama. He was never home with us, there was constant streams of credit card bills coming in the house with hotel charges on them and even my mama's best friend Gayle tried to put her up on some shit she heard from a reliable source. My mama dealt with the shit because of the constant flow of money but she was miserable. I saw her throw herself at any man that got close enough to her to smell her perfume. She had even messed with a few of my friends but I understood her pain being a married woman that was basically a single mother.

The few times I was around my father long enough to talk to him he just made it seem to me like getting money and getting women was what it was all about so I guess I bought into it. I always had at least three women in rotation at all times, that way when one messed up I always had another on to go to. It sounds fucked up but it worked for me. I had met Symphony before I ever laid eyes on Layla. My initial attraction to her was that she was older than me. She was dancing at a private party I went to over my nigga Mark's house. He had just turned 21 so we were all getting turned up. I was about to go home when he told me they had some dancer's coming.

I took my second blunt to the face as I waited for the strippers. The basement was full to capacity of niggas smoking, drinking, rolling, and finding random females to leave with. I never really felt comfortable being in Mechanicsville but I played it off. These nigga would trip if they came out to North Atlanta to see how I really lived. I was 15 and just stared really hanging in the studios with the older niggas.

"Aye you want another beer bruh?" Jay Dubb offered on his way to the over stocked bar in the corner. I knew his ass needed to quit drinking because he was my ride but I didn't want to look lame so I accepted the nasty ass beer. I don't see how anybody could drink these things. Shortly I had to pee and was barely able to make it to the tiny bathroom without pissing on myself. After washing my hands I was irritated to find there were no paper towel so I wiped my hands on Mark's mama's decorative towels while I checked myself in the mirror.

Thanks to the hair on my face I never looked my age. I had probably been in more clubs that a lot of these grown niggas had been in. When I opened the door I accidentally bumped whoever was standing in front of it. I was about to apologize because I knew how serious of an offense that was when my attention was directed to an ass bouncing in front of me. Apparently I had bumped one of the strippers while she was doing her thing to one of our new songs called "She's Beat."

Not having enough room to get past her I just stood there while went from grinding on me to doing the splits. I was mesmerized at the chocolate beauty in the Brazilian hair wig that I could tell had ran her a nice amount of bread. The star shaped leopard print pasties and leopard left nothing to the imagination as niggas threw all their bill money and child support on her. One nigga had even throw down his food stamp card. After her set was over I was finally able to make it back to my seat. She had bought three of her girls with her but none of them was bad as she was.

"Damn young nigga, I saw you over there getting your private session."

I laughed at Jay Dubb. I couldn't lie my dick was hard as life lesson as I watched her walking around talking to niggas not caring that she was damn near naked. She walked around to our table with a towel wrapped around her neck. We stared up at her but it was my and that she grabbed and pulled onto the dance floor. I was slightly terrified when I realized she was taking me outside. I had heard about strippers setting niggas up to get robbed. She walked to the side of the house before letting my hand go.

Pulling her hair out of her face she slit her eyes at me. "How old are you boy?"

"I'm old enough to be here. You brought me outside for a reason and it wasn't to ask about my age. "

She laughed flashing me a set of beautiful white teeth. I was expecting her to be all over me like her home girls on the inside of the party but all she wanted to do was talk to me. After that we were inseparable. She was my first which made me believe I could get her to stop dancing. Little did I know she was 5 years older than me and set in her ways. Before I knew it she was falling into the same shit her home girls were on. I had to hide my wallet when I spent the night with her and more and more pain pill prescriptions where strewn all over the floor. I even started hearing about her selling pussy which was the first time I ever put my hands on her. I spent the night with her while mama was out of town. I could never bring myself to come to the club where she danced at so I stayed at her crib while she worked.

I sat there all night waiting in her crib but she never showed and didn't answer her phone. My first thought was a nigga had done something to her. The sound of the front door creaking open. I sat up in the bed rubbing my eyes.

"Hey baby." She casually greeted me.

Her clothes were on backwards and makeup smeared everywhere. She looked like she had been rode hard and out up wet. I just sat on the edge of the bed staring at her.

"Sorry I didn't come home last night but we got caught up at work."

I almost laughed in her face. How do you get caught up at a strip club? It ain't like she was punching a time clock. I could feel myself starting to get worked up as she started taking her clothes off.

"So you couldn't call me and let me know you were okay? You let me sit here all night waiting on you?"

She tied her hair up in a scarf and proceeded to get in the bed behind me while I was talking to her.

"My phone was dead baby. Can we talk about this later because I am so tired?"

Because I knew I was already mad I just eased into to the living room to give her some space. As I settled onto the couch a shiny gold wrapper caught my attention. I wish I had just left it alone but I got up to grab what was an empty condom wrapper. It would've been cool if we used condoms but I had never used one before, not even the first time. I crept back in the bedroom to find her texting when she had just been too sleepy to talk to me. I asked her about the condom and she denied it which set me off. At first it was a little slap to make her stop lying then I choked *her. She apologized to me and we went on from there but it created a problem with my hands.*

Eventually we went our separate ways and I met Layla. The sex was so good with Symphony that I kept her around for that but we would never be back together. When I met Mona-Lisa I thought I would quit dealing with her but we still messed around on occasion. She was pissed when I started messing with Marissa though because she felt like she was too young but pussy is pussy to me as long as it has hair on it. Plus she carried herself like a woman in my opinion. Symphony would mean mug her at the studio but knew better than to say anything out of the way. When all the shit went down with me and Mona and Delano pulled that shit with the club I put Symphony in place to get close to the nigga. She was supposed to be helping me rob he nigga but the bitch was moving too slow.

It wasn't until I got real desperate for money that I realized I could use Marissa. By her being Mona's sister he would never look at her as being grimy. I had black-mailed her true enough but she didn't even realize I had already sold her little sex tape to a homegrown porn site. I thought I would have the time to lure him somewhere the night she told me she talked to the nigga. Who knew he would get in his feelins and react so

quickly?

Now I was up in here not even able to piss on my own. My mama was

crying and falling all over me like she cared so much and I was shocked my

father even bothered to show his face. The nigga only ever came around

when there was some kind of tragedy. These detectives was in my face every

time I opened my eyes which was getting old. The only thing I wanted to do

was get back to the studio. That nigga Delano's day would come soon

enough and it wouldn't be inside of a courtroom. Marissa wasn't off the

hook either because I feel like she fucked up the game plan on purpose.

These dicks weren't about to get a word outta me. As far as they know I got

a long list of enemies and anybody could have done this shit to me. Me and

Delano just had the most publicized beef because I blasted his punk ass

every chance I got.

"Mr. Waters how you feeling?"

The blonde nurse walking into my room looked like a chick I saw in a

porno once. The Atlanta A's scrubs she wore fit way tighter than they

should have. Her hands felt like clouds as she rubbed my arm.

"I am sore as hell but ok."

Like the doctor had warned I was quick to get out of breath and had to keep my sentences short. Every time I spoke it felt like somebody was tightening a string around my lungs. I had tried explaining that to the detectives but they weren't hearing it. After taking my blood pressure she checked my bandages. I never looked down to survey the damage but I knew it was bad from the way other people reacted. Mama damn near passed out the other day. My father sat in his chair giving off the vibe that he had somewhere else he would rather be. He barely even looked over at me the whole time he was there.

"Do you think you are up for some company?"

All I wanted to do was sleep. Besides my parents Marissa was the only person that had been to see me but I wasn't even awake while she was here. The only people it could be was the detectives but they never announced their visits they just came in.

"Who is it?"

The nurse walked into the hall returning a few seconds later. "There's a guy name Courtney here to see you. He says that you refer to him as Cash."

That was the last person I was expecting to see or hear from. "Send him in." I answered wondering what this nigga could possibly want with me.

I felt slightly guilty about what I had done to Marissa. She didn't deserve to find out the truth like that but it was all out in the open now. I was worried about her getting pulled over though because she didn't have a license. She had a way of finding trouble or letting trouble find her so after much debate I knew what I had to do. I called up Leslie who finally answered. After telling her what was up she was all game for going to help me find Marissa. She was always up for anything that might have the slightest chance of causing drama. I pulled up to her house shaking my head as she walked out of the door with a Newport hanging from her lip. I know her grandmother had to be sleep but then again she did all types of ratchet stuff right in front of her.

"Let's ride bitch!" She yelled putting on her seat belt.

"Girl why are you so turnt? We are just goin to look for my sister please calm yourself. Plus what kind of thug put's on a seatbelt anyway?"

"Girl you never know what might go down that's why I grabbed my granddaddy's 22 from under the bed."

"What the hell do we need a gun for?" I asked panicking.

"Girl you never know what could happen. You know Marissa likes to hang in the hood."

Nervously I pulled out of the driveway. My mind kept making me feel like she was somewhere where she could possibly hurt herself. Marissa was a very emotional person and she was fuming when she left the house. For all I know she could be somewhere wrapped around a tree. Her best friend Veronica was not the best example because she was always somewhere doing the most. I remembered when I first met her. She came over to the house in a sports bra and some gym shorts that were doing the most camel-toe. She was stacked like Buffy at the bottom and Dolly at the top. Her black and red taper was cute and her makeup done to perfection like she had her own personal makeup artist. She licked her lips at Daddy because he answered the door in his wife-beater and jogging pants. Immediately he turned his nose up at her before calling Marissa downstairs.

I knew she was the reason that Marissa had gotten down here and lost her mind. She lived with her older sister and three brothers. Nobody ever know what the hell happened to their parents. They didn't half ass go to school except for Veronica who used somebodies' address near our school zone so she could have a chance at a decent education. The girl was brilliant and beautiful but she just lacked home-training. She had a real bad reputation for selling her body, drinking, smoking, and anything else her young as had no business doing.

"You got any idea where we going Mo?

I had forgot all about Leslie as I had drifted off into my daydream.

"The first spot I thought about checking was Leslie's house."

Leslie turned her nose up. "We goin to Bankhead? I told you we would need this gun," she remarked patting the pouch of her hoodie.

"That's the only place I know of that she would go to. I don't know where any of her little friends stay at."

The backlight from Leslie's phone illuminated the entire front of the car. As she scrolled through her phone all I could think about was how I would be blamed if something happened to Marissa. I don't know what had gotten into daddy but the way he had treated her today let me know my time was up as favorite. I turned on the radio finding my boo Drake rapping about going from 0 to 100. I was at my favorite art when Leslie cut the sound down which got her a mean mug from me.

"We need to hit *Diamonds of Atlanta* right now."

"Why do we need to go to a strip club? Right now is not the time to be turning up Leslie."

I was beyond irritated now because all she thought about was partying. She never took a break from wanting to be somewhere drunk or either halfway there.

"Girl I just checked Marissa's face book page and she just checked in there about 20 minutes ago."

That was all she had to tell me. I turned the radio back up letting my foot slam down on the gas. Leslie gave me a horrified look and shouted something I paid no attention to. I was on a mission to save this girl from herself.

****

"Les do you see a blue Mustang anywhere? I enquired looking for somewhere to park. She obviously didn't hear me as she observed the hordes of half-naked women clamoring to get inside the club. I had never seen so much weave and booty in the same place.

"Leslie!" I yelled causing her to jump.

"Damn Mo I heard you the first time. I don't see a Mustang but I do see something, or rather somebody that I never expected to see out here.

"Who is it?"

"Correct me if I'm wrong but ain't that Marissa right there?"

I slammed the brakes almost causing us to be rear-ended by the car behind us. As he angrily blew on his horn I stared across the street at my sister. She looked like a video vixen in her corral one sleeved dress that had the stomach cut out and the back dipping low enough to show her matching G-string. Her hair was a bright Kool-Aid red wig and the platform heels she wore displayed a pink light every step she took.

"You gonna make this dude behind us shoot if you don't keep it moving." Leslie warned. I circled around the block before finally finding somewhere to park. By the time we walked around to where we had seen Marissa she was no longer there.

"Damn what are we gonna do Les?" I was starting to feel defeated when a bright red wig in the parking lot caught my attention.

"There she is, come on Les." We maneuvered through the crowd to get closer to the black Infinity Q60 convertible. There was a thick crowd of dudes around the crowd that we had to damn near fight through to even get to the car. Marissa was bent over the side of the car with her ass on full display for anybody that would look as she twerked to *Say Yes* by Lil Corey.

The girls inside the car cheered her on as the dudes made it rain on her damn near bare ass.

"Yesssssssss get it bitch!" The driver of the car exclaimed exiting the car to grind on her from behind. My mouth dropped when I realized who she was and the look on Leslie's face indicated she was just as shocked as I was. Without another thought I snatched her off my sister looking her dead in her face.

"So this is what you do? I knew your nasty ass couldn't be trusted!" Marissa turned around with her eyes bucked in fear. I snatched her arm pushing her into Leslie.

"Hold up you got her fucked up!" Veronica yelled jumping out of the car. She looked like she was 25 years old in her sequined bikini top and satin booty shorts. She called herself getting in my face so I swung on her and it was on. The crowd didn't make it no better as they hyped up the fight. She grabbed my hair like I knew she would but I grabbed her neck ramming her into the car where she continued to swing wildly never connecting with anything. I could feel my hair being ripped from my roots but didn't really care as I kept connecting with her chest and stomach.

Tearing her top off I threw it in the crowd for the greedy ass niggas that had crowded around trying to get a free thrill.

Veronica was so busy trying to keep her breast covered that she couldn't help but catch every punch. She screamed for help but nobody came to her aid. I think I took out all of my frustration on that little girl. She finally had the good sense to kick me with all her strength which sent me flying into the crowd where I was lifted off of my feet throwing me over his shoulder. I was about to swing on him when a familiar braid stopped me before I could start. The crowd slowly parted to let us through as I heard police sirens. Everybody scrambled to get to their cars. Setting me on my feet next to his car Delano opened his car door. He didn't say a word but I knew he was pissed. He waited for me to take my seat before gently closing the door.

"Aye grab her sister and Leslie's big mouth ass before the police lock em up!" He yelled to Cash.

Delano pulled around the police and onto Marietta. He turned up Kevin Gates *I don't get tired.*

Mona was starting to really get on my nerves. Every time she was out of my presence she was in some bullshit like I dint have enough going on already. Me and Cash had been sitting outside the club when she pulled up. At first I didn't think it was her because a strip club was the last place I would expect to see her. I had called Symphony to see when she would be at work because I wanted to holla at her after and see where her head was. I hated to think she was trying to help Todd set me up but I need to know for myself before I acted on it. Imagine my surprise when Mona pulled up. Like I said I didn't believe it was here at first until she got out of the car.

"She was dressed nice but way too classy to be going into a strip club while Leslie was dressed like she came to fight with a hoodie on and some jogging pants. As soon as they headed to the parking lot me and Cash followed them and that's when all hell broke loose. I never thought I would see my girl out there fighting around in a parking lot like some hood rat. Looking at her with her head resting on the window made her seem like a whole different person. What was I gonna do with her?

Turning the radio down she looked at me, "Where are we going?

"I am taking you home. Where else would we be going?"

"Who is gonna drive my car? My sister is drunk plus she ain't got a license so how is she gonna get her car home."

"I already got it handled ma don't worry about it."

She folded her hands against her chest pouting. She was so damn cute but so childish, a little bit too childish for me.

"I don't even have my keys to get in the house so we gotta turn back around anyway."

"No we don't! We will sit there until somebody gets there to let us in!"

"Who are you hollerin at like that? My daddy don't even yell at me like that."

I took my eyes off of the road to look at her. "That's what's wrong with you. That spoiled little girl shit is getting on my nerves. It was cute for the first five minutes but now you getting on my nerves. I should be the one mad havin to snatch up my girl in a strip club parking lot. Damn I thought you had more class than that."

"So I guess you didn't see Symphony over there too. She was driving the car my sister was dancing on, matter of fact she was dancing too but you ain't gonna say nothing about that though."

"What do you want me to say Mona? She ain't my girl, she is just the girl you keep accusing me of. I don't expect a whole lot from her because I don't care about her. I don't lay dick to her. All I do is live with her and that shit ends tonight because now I see she can't be trusted. This bitch been telling me that she works at the hospital which is cool since she don't owe me no explanations but anybody lying about something petty is lying about something big." I rounded the corner to Mona's street and pulled into the driveway.

"I tried to tell you about her but you got mad at me."
I sighed leaning back in my seat. "I'm not about gonna argue with you about it. You told me and I didn't believe you. Unlike niggas you are used to dealing with I take people at face value until they prove otherwise. I took you at face value and you always walkin out on me like the white girl you look like. I got enough people in my life I can't depend on but I expected you to be different."

Her face softened as she took my hand. "Del I don't know how to really handle you. I am used to dealing with somebody so opposite. Todd was terrible to me. I mean he did some straight-up sneaky, nasty stuff to me and I took it because I don't even know what a real relationship is. Hell may mama and daddy can't stand each other and can barely stand me and Marissa. They messed both of us up being dysfunctional."

I grabbed her chin in my hand. "I understand that you got some scars but damn ma we all do. I just met the most beautiful woman I ever seen in my life but I can't feel nothing for her because she gave me up. I don't really know what the whole story is and it don't even matter but I let that hurt me too long. You can't keep running from me because of what somebody else did."

She laid in my arms as a car pulled in behind us. We both looked back to a blue car pull in behind us. Cash got out of the blue car walking up to tap on my window. "Aye bruh I need to holla at you real quick."

I got out of the car as Mona looked over at me. Following him to the car I had no idea what I would find. When the car was empty an uneasy feeling came upon me.

"Bruh I tried to grab her sister and.............." Cash's voice trailed off.

"What happened?"

"I turned my back for a second and she was gone. She left in a blue Mustang is all I know."

I rubbed my hands over my face as Mona stepped out of the car to see what was going on. "Where is Marissa and Leslie?" She enquired trying to look through Cash's dark tint.

I looked at Cash who wasn't doing a good job of hiding his expression.

"Oh my God don't tell me she got locked up. The last thing I need is for her to be in a detention center."

"She ain't locked up ma." The relieved look on Mona's face would be short lived and I dreaded giving her the bad news.

"Aye Cash I appreciate you comin through." I wanted him to be gone when I broke it to her. Taking the hint he dapped me up hitting Mona with a head nod before getting in the car.

"Come on Mona we need to ride real quick."

"Where are we going? Where is Marissa?"

I took a deep breath knowing I couldn't hide the truth anymore. "She drove off in her car."

"Del she was pissy drunk! Oh my God she is gonna kill herself!"

I was conflicted because I was not as concerned as I should have been. The way Marissa had played me had left a bad taste in my mouth about her but seeing Mona worried outweighed all of that. When I was able to calm her down enough to get in the car she realized that she didn't have her phone so I gave her mines. We sat in the driveway as she waited for Marissa to answer.

"I went to voicemail, let me call Leslie to see if she tried to call me."

I was never one to panic but I knew that this didn't look good. She called Leslie but never got an answer.

"Calm down we just gonna go over there and see if your car is there. Mona leaned on my arms as we took the short drive to Leslie's house. As soon as we got around the corner we could see her car in Leslie's driveway. Now I was starting to think some shot was really up since she hadn't answered the phone.

"Why didn't she answer my calls if she got my car here?" Mona questioned reaching for the door handle.

"Stay in here I'm about to go knock on the door." I walked up to the front door noticing a TV turned on in the living room. I could make out Leslie sitting on the couch talking on the phone but as soon as I started knocking she cut it off like I didn't see her in there. Looking back at Mona I started beating on the door. After a few seconds I was about to kick the muthafucka in when it flew open. Leslie was standing there with her hair all over her head rubbing her eyes. *I know this bitch ain't tryna act like she was sleep.*

"Are you crazy beating on my door like that?" For good measure she stifled a yawn. Some weird shit was definitely goin down. Something told me not to mention Marissa to her.

"I came to get Mona's keys and phone from you. She tried calling you from my phone but I guess you was sleep."

"Okay but you didn't have to beat on my door like that. Where is Mona at anyway? You just scooped her and left everybody else to get locked up."

She fell asleep in the car. I was trying to get her out of there because I know those girls would've jumped her. I was wondering why you stood there and didn't help like you always do. We all know how much you love drama." She rolled her eyes. "So can I get her keys or are you gonna talk to me all night?" She smirked at me.

"Let me see what I did with em." She disappeared into the house closing the door after her but I watched her through the window. Mona opened the car door but I held my hand up to let her know I was good. She took her time looking upstairs so I opened the front door. Right on the arm of the couch was her phone with the backlight still lit. She had somebody on the phone. I could hear the floor creaking above me as I slid over to the couch. All I wanted to do was see who was on the phone but when I heard her coming down the steps I slid it in my pocket in time in enough time to land on the porch.

"Here is her stuff tell her to call me in the morning." I didn't even have a chance to say thank you before she was locking the door in my face. I ran back to the car peeling out before she noticed the phone was missing.

"What was all that about?" Mona questioned annoyed.

"I don't know what your girl is on but she was definitely acting weird as hell."

"Weird how?"

"I will explain later just grab these keys and go straight home. I'ma follow you and wait until you get in."

I stood there for a second not knowing what to think.

"Get in the fuckin car Mona!"

Without knowing why I was doing it I got in the car pulling out with Delano trailing me. I thought I saw Leslie run out on her porch in my rearview but maybe I was just imagining things.

As soon as I pulled up to my house Delano got out walking me to the door. "I don't know what your girl is on but you need to leave that bitch alone."

"What are you talking about? Why don't you just tell me what happened Del?"

"I will do all that later but right now I need you to get in the house and make sure the alarm is on. I'm about to go find your sister and bring her home but I need you to be safe."

The look in his eyes was scaring me but I didn't want to question him. I wanted to find Marissa before daddy got off of work because once he got wind of everything that happened there was no telling what he would do with his terrible temper. Delano walked inside of the house with me checking every room. I didn't know what he was looking for but I also knew I didn't want to be in this house by myself. Satisfied that the coast was clear he grabbed my shoulder bending down to look in my eyes. "Don't leave this house I'm dead serious. I will handle everything but I need you to stay here in case she comes back."

"Del you are scaring me. Do we need to call the police?"

"No because we don't even know what's goin on yet. Just stay here and I will call you as soon as I know something." He kissed me softly before walking out of the front door. I hurriedly locked up behind him feeling paranoid. Staring out of the living room door until he drove off I retrieved my phone from my pocket. Marissa still wasn't answering. I debated whether or not to text daddy at work but decided not to get him worked up until I knew something for sure. The only friend she had that I knew how to get to was Veronica. I know I promised Delano I wouldn't leave but I had to find her. He probably wouldn't even look for real since he didn't like her. Sitting down on the couch I turned on the TV and of course the first thing I saw was the news. It seemed like every channel I turned to was playing some type of crime drama or documentary which made me even more afraid that she was hurt. Looking at my keys laying on the coffee table I knew what I had to do.

Taking one more look out of the front door to make sure Delano didn't circle the block I disarmed the alarm stepping out onto the porch. It was pitch black outside making me wish I had turned on the porch light but I didn't have the time to worry about it now. After locking the door I walked over to my car getting inside. Taking a deep breath I turned the key in the

ignition. No matter what Del said, I had to go to Bankhead to find my sister.

My head felt like lead as I tried to get comfortable in the chair. The clicking of Symphony's heels was killing me. With my hands bound behind me I was defenseless to her numerous kicks and punches.

"You wanna tell me again who you been runnin your mouth to or you gon make me beat your ass some more?"

"I didn't tell nobody nothing I swear."

"You didn't tell nobody nothing huh? How Delano getting all his information? I see you didn't run down to the police station when my man got shot to talk to them but you can talk to the enemy."

The pain in my head and stomach where she had hit me numerous times was no match for the fear I had of not making it out of here alive. I looked around Veronica's basement knowing it would be the last place I ever saw. I couldn't believe how easily they had played me.

After leaving mama my mind was messed up. I called up Veronica to see what she was doing so that I could try to salvage my birthday. When she said she was free we agreed to meet at the strip club because that's where all the ballers and bread winners hung out at. My wounded state of mind clouded my better judgment so I went the adult book store and grabbed the sluttiest outfit I could find to put on. My body had always made me feel good about myself because I had what so many were going out buying. Even Veronica had gotten ass shots a few times from her cousin. When I met up with them at the club I was a little put off to see Symphony with her. I knew I had seen her before but couldn't place where because she looked so different with the short, natural hair.

Since the parking lot was fat we sat in Symphony's car while she let the top down. None of the bitches looked better than us not even the strippers. Soon the pills and drinks started flowing and even though I wasn't feeling it I allowed Veronica talk me into drinking something she had missed up in a Grey Goose bottle. I thought it was cool since we all were drinking from the same bottle or so I thought we were anyway. I was on one by the time Mona came snatching me up. She was always trying to be a party pooper like and old ass woman so yeah I was mad when she snatched me up. Plus, with the crowd of nigga we had throwing money I know we could have easily made a stack out there. I was shocked when she fought Veronica because Mona had never been the type to fight. Leslie was usually the ratchet one but it was like she stood there laughing the whole time. When Delano threw Mona over his shoulder I knew it was my cue to leave too. He yelled something to somebody but everybody went crazy when the police pulled up.

I was too drunk to even find my car so Symphony grabbed me pushing into her car before she peeled out. I was knocked out by the time I got to Veronica's house. As soon as we were inside the dragged me down the basement throwing me into this chair. Veronica took the chain they used to use on their Blue pit to chain my hands behind my back then she left me in the basement with this crazy bitch. Yeah I knew when she told me who she was, I would die in here.

"You young, dumb, full of cum and don't know nothing about life. What did he even want you for when he had a woman? Plus what kind of woman takes her sister's leftovers? I guess it's true, these hoes ain't loyal." She smiled as she walked past me to a jug that was sitting on the floor. It looked like a bleach jug but I wasn't sure as my eyes were starting to swell shut. The splash of liquid that hit my face was much worse than bleach, it was gasoline. "Oh I'm sorry I thought you liked getting splashed on, at least that's what I saw in one of your videos."

"Please let me go, I didn't tell nobody nothing." I whispered.

"Naw you didn't tell nobody directly but you sent Tay up there to run his mouth. I told Todd you liked that ugly ass nigga but he didn't listen."

I was stunned because I hadn't seen or heard from Tay since the night he took me home. I had even tried looking him up of face book but I didn't know his real name.

"I-I-I- didn't tell him nothing I swear. I haven't even seen him."

She yanked my head wrapping her hands around my hair. So you mean to tell me that the nigga left Detroit to come down here and just so happened to run into Cash? Is that what you want me to believe? Then on top of that I had to keep dealing with your sister? I warned you that she had it coming if she kept fuckin with me. She was worried about me taking her lil boyfriend when you was the one that really wanted him."

Her words stung like acid because she was right. I wanted Todd, Delano, and basically everything that Mona-Lisa had but I never expected it to end like this. I knew Symphony was crazy about Todd and willing to do any and everything in her power to get him to herself. No amount of pleading or begging would change her mind.

"I almost feel sorry for you because I remember what you told me and Veronica about not being loved by your family. We went through the same thing which is why I ended up raising my brothers and sister. Todd was the only thing I had to myself or so I thought until I found out about all his sidelines. Don't worry though, because after you are gone so is your sister and that bitch Layla I will save for last since she has given me the most headache."

My stomach was a mass of knots as she started rummaging through a duffle bag she had on the floor. I would have preferred a painless death if it were up to me. After watching a scary movie as a child one of my worst fears was being burned alive. In the movie the girl ran back into her house to save her dog but never came out. She was horribly disfigured when they brought her body out of the house. This girl wanted to make sure I was not able to be recognized because she hated me so much. The crazy thing is I never even knew she had feelings for Todd when I first started hanging with her.

"Why do you wear weave when you got all this pretty hair?" Symphony finger combed my hair while we waited on Veronica to get ready. As usual she never knew which shoes she wanted to wear. She had boosted so many pair that her closet looked like the inside of a Payless.

"It's long but not as full as I would like it plus my mama would have a fit if I tried to color my real hair." As soon as Symphony turned her back

I fluffed my curls up where she had flattened them. I was starting to wonder if she had secret feelings because earlier she tried to get me to wear a dress that was shapeless and big. She had a banging body too so she couldn't have been worried about me outshining her. She was bald-headed though I couldn't deny that but she seemed to like the Amber Rose look and she pulled it off well.

"Come on Veronica, I still gotta stop by my crib and grab some more outfits for tonight."

Veronica frowned but finally settle on a pair of suede purple pumps. "Ok dang Sym you could have done all that first instead of rushing me." She adjusted the studded tube top she had on before pulling the high-waisted mini skirt up. "I know you just wanna get some from Todd before we go out, you ain't slick."

I pretended not to hear what she said but my heart dropped a little. It was not too long ago we had all went to Layla's apartment to confront her about some threatening text she had sent me. Symphony stepped in like a big sister but now I see she had her own agenda in wanting to confront her. She had never acted like anything more than a friend to Todd. We had all been around each other on several occasions but there was never flirting, or any other gesture to give the impression that they were anything more than that. Veronica always said he was like a brother to them which now made sense if he was fucking her sister.

I don't know why I felt worse about having sex with Todd in regards to her than I did about Mona. I guess with Mona it was more of a revenge thing because of my jealousy but with Symphony I felt sorry for her. Her whole world was her sister and three brothers. Todd was very controlling and manipulative but I couldn't imagine him having enough power to make this woman keep quiet about her position in his life. Maybe he was slinging the dick as good to her as he was to me. I know it wasn't that he spoiled her so well because he made it clear to me a long time ago that he only tricked on Layla and I had recently been going into mama's purse to steal money for him. He was like a drug and I was addicted. Now I was starting to wonder if he was messing with Veronica too.

I had to learn the hard way not to put anything past him. I couldn't even concentrate that night as I danced. I kept messing up my pole tricks and dancing offbeat so I knew my money would be short. Todd had already been threatening to sell the sex tape of him and his friends running through me while I was high out of my mind. The small part of it that he showed me was completely degrading. It was out of this desperation that I came up with the plan to rob Delano. Todd wasn't *really into the idea of being put in it but I knew it was the only way to get to Delano. He was gone off of Mona so by me being her sister he would also have to show here he cared about me.*

The way it was supposed to go down was I would tell Delano when Todd was somewhere by himself so he could go confront him. As soon as Delano got there I would have people waiting to rob him. Well Delano took it upon himself to just go to him without waiting for my call which was where everything went wrong.

The smell of smoke brought me out of my daze. Symphony had left me in the basement alone turning out the lights. It was pitch black except the small light let in through the window. I struggled with the chair but couldn't make the chains budge. I guess this was what I deserved for being so low-down to Mona who I now see didn't deserve this. Closing my eyes tightly I tried to calm my breathing to keep from taking in too much of the noxious fumes which were getting closer. The fire had been set upstairs trapping me. I was about to die in a basement chained up like a prisoner.

After leaving Mona's I stopped to get some gas as well as look through Veronica's phone. Going back through her call log I see she had a lot of calls from numbers that weren't locked into her phone, for me that was a red flag. I googled the last number that she called and saw that it came from Bankhead. Thinking back to earlier I remembered that her, Symphony, and her little sister Veronica were the last people seen with Marissa. All we knew is that she drove off but had no idea who she drove off with. I started to call Mona and ask her if she had Veronica's address but didn't want to alarm her. Knowing Mona all she would do was overreact and call the police. After thinking for a quick second I decided to look into the GPS. There were four different addresses there but only one in Bankhead which I hoped was the right one. Following the directions I made my way to the highway immediately jumping in the fast lane. Something told me that this wouldn't end well.

I had to be doing every bit of 90 swerving in and out of lanes trying to get there. As much as I hated Marissa for what she did to me all I could think about was how Mona would feel if something happened to her. She had told me more than a few times how close they used to be before they moved here. They used to go everywhere and do everything together. I always wished I had a brother or sister to share my childhood with. Every fight I got in I go into on my own. Every secret I had I kept to myself because I wasn't able to trust anybody. Just like I thought about Mona's feelings when I shot Todd I was thinking about them now. Glancing at the GPS I saw my exit coming up so I swerved over four lanes almost colliding with another car to make sure I made it.

Pulling up in front of a yellow house I checked the address to make sure I had it right because it appeared that nobody was at home. Parking across the street I grabbed my glock from the console before exiting the car. The grass was wet causing me to damn near slip as I ran up. *Who the fuck runs their sprinklers at night time?* The acrid smell of smoke filled the air but it was so dark on the street I couldn't see where it was coming from until I ran up to the porch peering into the front window. I could see flames everywhere. I ran to the back of the house where I saw a blue car driving down the narrow alley. I couldn't make out the model because of how fast the car was going but I knew it had to be Marissa's car.

Looking around both ways I carefully walked up to the back door looking through the glass. I could see smoke but still no sign of where the fire was. Breaking the glass with my gun I unlocked the door letting myself in. Immediately I dropped low to keep from choking. With the door sitting wide opened it let out a lot of the smoke. I crawled through the broken glass not even worrying about cutting my hands. Once I made it to the hallway there were three doors ahead of me. As I pushed open each door two of them revealed bedrooms while the other was a bathroom. They were all empty. As a matter of fact the whole house unfurnished like somebody had just moved out as empty boxes sat in piles on the floor.

Crawling into the living room I could see the source of the fire. Somebody had stuffed newspaper into a space heater. I knew I didn't have time to look for a fire extinguisher and water was the worst thing to put on an electrical fire. As I tried not panic my mind recalled being in Cash's house which was made very similar to this. On his basement wall there was a shelf on the stairwell which held a fire extinguisher. Although my lungs were burning I had to see if there was a basement. Staying as low to the ground as I could I made my way back into kitchen. Fumbling around on the floor I searched for an opening for another door in the kitchen but couldn't find one. Time was running out as my breathing became increasingly heavier. Feeling defeated I crawled towards the back door when looked back realizing the fridge was in the wrong place.

That refrigerator is blocking something! Summoning my last bit of strength I pushed the refrigerator out of the way to reveal a door knob. Opening the door I yelled down into the basement as the smoke started to fill up the space behind me. I grabbed the fire extinguisher off the side wall but was consumed by the black smoke as I turned around. Right now the choice was grim. Either I could run back and try to put out the fire or walk down these steps to see if Marissa was in here. With the extinguisher still in hand I ran down the steps feeling on the walls for a light switch. When I finally found it Marissa was in the center of the floor slumped over in a chair.

There was no time to waste knowing this house was burning right above our heads. The windows were too small to crawl out of so I was gonna have to take her back up the steps. The chains fastened around her arms were too tight to even think about sliding her out. I tried shaking her but she wouldn't respond so I knew I would have to do this by myself. With throat burning and eyes watering I grabbed the chair hoisting it as best as I could over my shoulders and started back up the steps. The flames were in the kitchen as I realized I had left the extinguisher in the basement.

Feeling myself growing weaker I took the best aim I could throwing Marissa out of the narrow doorway. If she broke and arm that was the least of my worries. My chest began to burn as I contemplated trying to run through the flames. I could feel my legs crumble underneath me. Sirens rang out in the distance but it was too late.

Chapter 27

Mona-Lisa

Veronica's street was a mixture emergency vehicles. The police, fire truck, and ambulance all congested the narrow area. I had to park at least 8 houses down. I could smell smoke the moment I stepped out of my car. There were people everywhere observing the scene as the firemen raced to put out the fire. At first I couldn't tell which house it was but the closer I got the more my heart dropped. I spotted a car very similar to Delano's but surely he wouldn't be in this area. I could hear wailing from a woman as the police held her back. As I approached the house all I could see were the skeletal remains of it. The unfamiliar woman continued to yell and scream making me wonder who she was.

"Ma'am you have to stand back and let the firemen work." The officer said trying to comfort her. "I been knowing those kids all their life and they didn't have nobody. They mama and daddy just left em to raise theyselves. I know I shoulda called the child protection peoples but I would see about em when I could." She continued to cry as the police officer led her away through the crowd. My heart sank. If Veronica was dead then where was my sister?

"Hey let them through!" An officer yelled as a stretcher was being wheeled from around the house. The nosey crowd still stood there straining to see who was on the bed. I could make out a girl from the long hair but her face was covered with an oxygen mask. I strained to see more when I was able to make out the earrings that Marissa had on.

"Oh my God that is my sister!!!!" I ran up to the ambulance as they were loading her in. An officer grabbed me but I fought with him, "That is my little sister!" "Ma'am you have to calm down." He asserted spinning me around. "If this is your sister the last thing we need right now is for you to panic okay?" I tried to listen to him but my concentration was broken by the sounds of the paramedics. I kept hearing them mentioning shallow breathing. I looked around the officer as another stretcher came from around the house. I couldn't make out if the person's face was covered by the sheet or not. The one thing I could see clearly was a single braid. My legs folded under me like a card table.

Chapter 28

My right arm was a mass of tubes as I tried to roll over. I woke up in a white room with a light so bright in my face that I thought I was in Heaven, I waited for the harps and violins to start playing but when I saw daddy's face I knew I was in hell.

"Baby girl you are finally awake. How do you feel?" Him rubbing my bandaged head was somewhat scary as I couldn't recall the last time he touched me. I tried to speak but no words came out. My throat felt like the Sahara desert plus I was hindered by my oxygen mask. He continued to stroke my head.

"Jill come here she is woke." He held his hand out for mama a she walked up to my bed slowly. Her green eyes were red rimmed from crying. She leaned over kissing my forehead. I wondered where Mona was because I needed to see her. I need her to know that I was truly sorry for everything I had done to her.

"Are you able to talk?" Mama asked lifting the mask from my face. I shook my no as she carefully lowered it back down. Hugging daddy she softly cried into his chest. If I knew it would take all this for them to act decent towards each other I would have probably did something to myself a long time ago. Mona appeared in the doorway looking like she had been through a hurricane. She still wore the dress from my birthday dinner but instead of heels she wore hospital footies. She had a wristband on her arm letting me know she had been admitted too. Seeing my eyes open she broke down crying which made me cry. She hugged me as tightly as she could with the IV in the way.

"I was so scared I was gonna lose you. Why you leave like that Rissa? You could have killed yourself. What happened with the fire? Where is Veronica?"

As much as I wanted to answer her questions I just didn't have the speaking voice. I wanted to tell her and everyone all that had happened but I simply didn't have the voice. Daddy had to grab her off of me because she was squeezing my tubes. He got her to take a seat and kneeled in front of her. I couldn't hear what he was saying but it seemed to calm her down.

Mama stood there holding my hand. "I feel like this is all my fault. I was so caught up in what I had going on that I completely lost sight of being a mother. After what I told you last night I knew you was upset and I should've never let you leave in that condition. I don't know what I would do if something ever happened to you or Mona." She whispered. "I messed up this while family and I know I have got to fix it but you have to give me a chance baby. I just need one more chance to fix this." Her tears dripped from her eyes falling onto our interlocked hands, I didn't know how much more of this I could take but thankfully a doctor appeared knocking on the door. "Hello folks I am Dr. Gerard and I take it you are family?"

Daddy walked up shaking his hand. "Yeah this is me, my uh wife, and my two daughters." "Oh, well great to meet you I just hate it was under such unfortunate circumstances. I just wanted you all to know that we are still going to be running tests but she won't be able to speak for a while. There was some damage to her windpipe due to the smoke inhalation which has caused her breath to be very short. If she were not on oxygen right now she would sound like a person having an asthma attack." He walked over to me grabbing my hand. "Are you in any type of pain right now?" My back was killing me and my hands were still sore from where they had been bound. I shook my head yes. "Okay well we will be in momentarily to do run some more tests and then you will be able to get some pain medicine. I know that what has happened has been traumatic but I really think it best to let her get some rest as you all should too."

"Naw I'm not trying to leave her up here by herself until I know what happened at that house." Daddy stated firmly. "May I have a word with you sir?" Daddy looked around at us before walking out of the room. They closed the door behind them so we had no idea what they were saying. Mona was texting furiously on her phone. She was probably telling Delano what was going on. Mama just rubbed my arm looking off into space. She was really starting to scare the hell out of me.

"Okay so I talked to the doc and the police are gonna be up here. We need to go home but we will be back first thing in the morning." Nobody protested as they all looked tired. Mona pulled my mask down to kiss me on the cheek." Dr. Gerard turned the lights off after them and I found my way somehow to a little bit of a peaceful sleep.

My mind was a mass of thoughts as I called Delano for the hundredth time. His phone was still turned off. *Why did they take him to a different hospital?* I had no way of getting in touch with his father because I didn't have his number. I really didn't want to ask mama for it either. "Baby girl do you want to go get your car tonight or wait until the morning?" Daddy asked. I thought about it and if I grabbed my car I could go ahead and go to his father's house in case he hadn't heard what happened. "I wanna go ahead and get it tonight." As much as I dreaded seeing that house again I need to know where my baby was.

My hands shook as we pulled up to the scene. There was still so much smoke and soot in the distance as officers and firemen where still out there. Daddy walked me to my car as I looked up the street as Delano's Camaro. I felt so heavy as I slid into my car. "Make sure you follow us home baby girl." Daddy kissed me on the forehead before closing my door. I waited for them to pull off and followed them on the highway. Daddy deliberately drove the speed limit to make sure I kept up with him but I was on a mission. I stayed behind them until I came to my exit and quickly got off. I could hear my phone ringing almost immediately and it was mama. I ignored her and kept going.

The sun had begun to come up There was a set of matching black Lincoln Navigators in the driveway so I knew someone was there. As I approached the house I could hear yelling. "All you were supposed to do was protect him! Was that so hard? I stayed away like you asked me to and now my son is laying in a damn hospital bed! How did you think I would react Dorian?" I was apprehensive about knocking on the door but I took a breath and did it anyway. A man standing at least 6'6 answered the door. With his dark hair and black suit he reminded me of Lurch from the Addams Family show I used to watch with granddaddy."

"Who is at the door Arnold?" The woman asked from inside of the house. "Who are you?" He asked repeating her question to me. "I'm Mona-Lisa, Delano's girlfriend." He eyed me up and down before opening the door all of the way. I felt like I walked in on the set of the Sopranos as I was surrounded by Italian men in suits. Six pairs of eyes followed me into the kitchen where Mr. Dawson with his head in his hands. The lady with dark hair standing on the side of him whipped her head in my direction revealing the most beautiful set of blue eyes. *Oh shit this is his mother.*

"Who are you?" I didn't know what to say as my mouth had went completely dry. "I-I am Mona-Lisa, Delano's girlfriend." Mr. Dawson looked up at me. "So you wanna tell me what happened to my damn son?!" He stood up looking down at me as she looked at me. It seemed like all sets of eyes were on me and I came here looking for answers too. I didn't know what to do but the tears in my eyes found their way down my face. "No why did you have to go and scare the poor girl?" She looked back at Mr. Dawson in disgust as she grabbed my hand. "Listen my dear I am Delano's mother and we are looking for him right now. We just left the scene of the fire and nobody seems to know what happened or what hospital he was taken to. You have to excuse his father's emotions right now he is just worried."

"Hold on I got a call!" Mr. Dawson yelled throwing up his finger to silence her. "Yes this is his father. Uh huh. Yeah I see. I will be on my way right now. Thank you so much!" He disconnected the call glaring at me, "They got him at Grady Memorial we need to leave now!" She let go of me barking orders to the men sitting in the living room. We all filed towards the door. "Where do you think you are going?" Mr. Dawson questioned me.

"She had every right to see about him being his girlfriend. She had even more right than me to be here so stop making an ass out of yourself." She grabbed my hand pulling me outside as one of the suited men held open the doors for us. I climbed in first feeling very uneasy. These dudes flanked her like she was a female president or something. Once we were safely inside she whispered another command to the driver who flipped open a huge GPS screen on the dashboard. The vehicle smelled like new leather as it intermingled with whatever fragrance she was wearing. "So Mona-Lisa like the painting. Tell me more about you. How did you meet my son?"

"We met at his nightclub. He used to work with my ex-boyfriend and sorta stepped in when we got into it." "Hmm so my son is chivalrous, he must have gotten that from Dorian." I kept trying to avoid her eyes at the seemed to stare right through me like he said. There was something a little familiar about her face but I couldn't place it. "So your ex-boyfriend is the little boy that got shot correct?" I nodded my head yes. "Hmm seems like I will have to teach him to have better aim in the future." A resounding chorus of laughter filled the truck but I didn't find anything funny. I didn't know who these people were but I knew they had to be dangerous.

"Why are you not laughing I am trying to lighten the mood." I stifled a smile. "Listen to me Bella, we are going to get to the bottom of this. I will not allow a hair on my sons head to be harmed and just stand by. I don't know what you have been told about me but believe only what you see."

After that she looked out of the window so I sat there figuring it was best not to ask too many questions. I had watched enough mafia movies to know that these people did not like to be asked a lot of questions. I wished I hadn't left my phone in the car because now I was at this woman's mercy. We rode the rest of the way in silence with the only sound coming from the GPS as it directed us to the hospital. When we arrived she jumped into action.

"Me and the girl will go in. I want you all to find the hospital entrances and secure them. They jumped out of the truck opening the doors for us before disappearing around the building. She answered a call on her phone as we walked into the hospital. There was a lot of whispering but I couldn't make out what she was saying. Even in the stilettos she wore she guided across the floor effortlessly. I could barely keep up with her steps with my short legs.

The waiting room was crowded as we stepped inside. This place looked more like a club than a hospital with all of the ridiculously dressed females sitting there. She told me to have a seat as she approached the check-in station. I was hesitant to sit down next to a man that had what appeared to be a stab wound on his side. He tried to find a comfortable position to sit in but nothing seemed to work for him. "Bitch got me in here waiting I'm near bout gon bleed to damn death for they get me some help."

I tried not to laugh but the look on his toothless face was priceless. I began

making up stories in my mind about the various injuries I saw so that I

could keep myself sane. I didn't know what type of condition Delano would

be in.

"Mona-Lisa let's go!" Everybody looked at me as I slowly walked to

wear she stood. Slapping a visitor sticker on my chest she led the way as we

got on the elevators. "I don't think I ever told you but my name is

Constantina. I know it is a long name but you can call me Connie since only

people I do not like call me Tina, capeesh?" "Yes ma'am." We got off of the

elevator as she gazed at the note in her hand. "This way Bella." I followed

her down a seemingly endless maze of corridors until she stopped in front

of a closed door. She pulled out her necklace chanting a short prayer before

kissing it. When we got inside Delano was sitting up watching TV. His arm

was bandaged heavily in gauze and there were cuts on his face. His hair was

wet and clinging to his shoulders.

In my haste to hug him I grabbed his sore arm causing him to wince.

"Be careful ma I got a bit of a burn goin on right there. He kissed me

grabbing me with his other arm that was only in slightly better condition.

"Hello son." He gave her a look before nodding his head. "I am glad that you're okay I was so worried about you." He sucked his teethe holding back the smart comment that I knew was on the tip of his tongue. ""What happened over there Del?" I questioned grabbing his face. "That is a long ass story that I have already recounted to the best of my knowledge. I want to get the fuck outta her so I can handle my business. Is your sister okay?" "Yeah she's okay. Don't you think you need to talk to your mother?" I whispered. Sighing he looked back at her holding his arms out. I moved so that she could hug him. I could tell the gesture meant a lot to her as she pulled back with tears in her eyes.

"Damn is it a family reunion in here?" Mr. Dawson bellowed from the door. He walked to the other side of the bed rubbing Delano's head. "Hey pops. I was wondering if you was coming." "Now why would you even wonder that? Just because we fell out don't mean you ain't still my son. Hell I been around you your whole life getting pissed off at you." That was an obvious dig to his mother but she didn't say anything. "I had to stop and get you something to eat. I know they gonna have some nasty ass food up in here." Delano reached for the greasy bag which his mother helped him open. "He gets burned and you bring him cheese steak and fries, you want him to have a heart attack to?"

"Tina don't start with me. I've had more than enough of your mouth this morning. You come up in my house with those fake ass gangsters like yall was about to do something to me." She placed her hands on her hips. "First of all nothing was fake about them and secondly don't use the term gangsters around me because you know I hate that. Their guns were very real and so was you fear so let's not put on airs for the children." Delano started laughing. "This shit is crazy. I am in here broke up and yall arguing. I need yall to take that out of here so I can eat my food in peace." She looked at Mr. Dawson as if challenging him. "Let's take this outside." Shaking his head he followed her out of the door. "You don't scare nobody Tina."

After the door closed Delano grabbed me close kissing me deeply. I was lying against his hot ass sandwich but didn't care. My tongue slid over his effortlessly as he ran his fingers through my now tangled curls. "Damn ma I thought I would never see you again. I gotta tell you I love you because it's something we don't say enough of." "I love you too Del but if you don't let me up I'm gonna be a burn victim too because this sandwich is hot as hell. He laughed releasing me. I fed him a piece of sandwich before taking a bite myself. "Now that they are gone can you tell me what happened?" Finishing the food in his mouth he gestured for the cup next to make.

After taking a sip he went on to tell me a very bizarre tale. This had all went so much deeper than I imagined it. Todd was a force to be reckoned with. I had no idea all that I had been exposed to being with him. He truly was the epitome of a snake not caring who he stepped on. I was wondering what Leslie's role was in all of this. We had never really fell out except for the brief time I had stopped dealing with her due to her ratchetness. We got back cool though so I thought we were good plus I apologized to her. It was funny she hadn't called until Delano told me that he had taken her phone. I had to laugh at that because he was determined to prove she was up to no good. He never liked me being around her to begin with.

"So what do we do with all of this information? I mean we can give it to the police but what can we prove? As far as I know they haven't found Marissa's car. All we know is that she left the club and went to Veronica's. She was probably mad at me because I kinda ruined her little birthday for her and that's what made her go to the club to begin with. Mama said she had saw her briefly after she left the house though. I am so confused." He shifted in the bed trying to get comfortable. "Don't worry ma we gonna figure all of this out just give me a second to think. I don't want the dick all over this because they are already looking at me for that shit with Todd."

I understood where he was coming from because this was a tangled mess. I had no idea how bad it would get but soon enough we would all find out.

Seeing Mona in good spirits had been worth all of the pain I was in. I never wanted to see tears paint her beautiful face again. However, I was not thrilled about my mother being here. She has dot have taken a red-eye to get here from NYC in time. I just felt like the woman had an agenda and I didn't want to know what it was. I watched everything she did. It wasn't lost on me that she had henchmen following her everywhere she went like some type of mafia princess. I thought about the day I bought the club with Todd. Mr. Ralph said it was going so cheap because it brought back bad memories of his sister getting 25 years for something. Either this woman got some bodies on her or she was in the dope game. Either way I wanted no parts of her. Nothing she could tell me could ever make up for not being a mother to me.

Right now I needed Cash to put his ear to the street for me. Even with him my mind was a little frayed because I knew he heard by now. He had to have known something went down. I'm sure the news had covered the story. I would never know because my phone was still in my car. I would have sent Mona to get it but I didn't want her anywhere near the police right now who had probably searched my shit anyway. "So what do you think about Constantina?"

"I think she is gorgeous. You told me she was beautiful but I had no idea she would look like that. She looks like a model." "Funny you should say that ma. You got your phone on you?" She patted her pockets. "No I left it in my car I'm sorry."

"No worries ma call the nurse for me." She grabbed the remote from my bed pushing the nurse call button. "Yes may I help you?" Mona looked at me. "Hey can I get a nurse real quick please, I need my bed lifted." "Yes sir we will send someone in shortly." A few seconds later a nurse walked in. "Yes sir you called?" She was smiling so hard at him that it took a second for her to even realize I was there. "I know this is gonna sound weird but do you have a phone?" She gave him a puzzled look. I have one but there is also one by your bed." "Oh I know but I need to look up something real quick on google."

She looked at me but I shrugged my shoulders. I didn't know what he was about to do. She slid her phone out of her pocket unlocking it before passing it to him. He typed in something and started scrolling. *I hope she ain't got no naked pictures in there.* I thought to myself. "Check this out ma." Delano said holding the phone up to my face. My mouth dropped as I grabbed the phone looking at what appeared to be a very young version of his mother in a bikini. The nurse looked over my shoulder as I looked at all of the other pictures of her. She apparently had been an internationally known supermodel. The men with her must have been her bodyguards. I handed the nurse back her phone. "I don't mean to be nosy but do you know her or something? She is very beautiful." Delano winked at me. "She is the mother of this dude I know." "Oh, well do you need anything else while I am in here?" "Nah, I think I am good right now but later I might need something for this arms because it's starting to hurt a little bit."

"I could give you something right now but it will make you sleepy." He waved her off, "I would rather wait until later." "Just let me know if you need anything." As soon as she exited I punched Delano's good arm. "Damn ma you gotta watch that shit I got shards of glass everywhere." "I'm sorry. Why didn't you tell me your mother was a model?" He scratched his head. "I didn't tell nobody. Ever since I met her I been trying to find out everything I can about her. She has modeled for Movado, Christian Dior, Pucci, and Versace but that's all I can seem to find out about her for real. I feel like she came back in my life for other reasons besides me being in trouble. I just don't trust her." I cupped his face in my hands. "I think we are both in a situation where we don't know who to trust. My parents been holding back their share of secrets too." "Like what?" He questioned just as

the door opened.

Constantina walked back in by herself which I took to be a bad sign. "Where did pops go?" She looked behind her before closing the door. "He is talking to detectives at the moment." I was definitely not trying to speak to a detective right now so I hoped they would leave it at that. "Mona can I please have a minute I would like to have a word with my son if I may." Mona looked into my eyes for approval before kissing my lips. As she passed I heard my mother whisper something to her that made her smile. "Delano I have to be very honest with you about somethings and now may be the best time for me to tell them to you. I think it is important to realize just who I am and why I really had to leave your life."

Great here go more secrets on top of all the other shit I got going on.

"I don't know where to start but I guess the beginning is the most suitable place. She sat on the edge of my bed rubbing my legs. "I am your mother none of that has been a fabrication but there are things about me and your father that you do not know and he asked me not to tell you however I cannot keep this myth going any longer." I braced myself for the worst because I knew it was coming.

"This is harder than I thought it would be. I need a cigar right about now." She laughed. "Anyway, I wanted to be in your life but I was already on the brink of a modeling career when I met Dorian. He was young and handsome and we had our thing which produced you. He was by far not ready to settle down and neither was I. Devastation was is not a strong enough word for the way I felt when I found out I was pregnant. I knew my father would never understand or approve. I also knew that when I didn't get to see Dorian for those few months that I would never accept his excuse. He really had gotten in trouble but I found that out much later. I had to be quarantined from my family in order to give birth to you. They were ashamed of a mixed baby destroying their bloodline so I had to get rid of you as quickly and safely as possible. I felt like Moses's mother as I handed you to my sister Rosaline who was moving here to go to medical school. She brought you here safely thinking that she would get to be in your life but your father never allowed that."

This was a lot to take in but what she said next would really fuck with my mind. "Rosaline unfortunately did not do well health wise and after being here a few short years she had died. We tried to bring her body back home to Italy but there was so much red tape to go through that we had to come here to bury here. As soon as I touched the soil to the place where my child was I knew I could never leave so I stayed here looking for you. I come from a very important family so I was easily able to get the connections to find you. The first time I saw you again you were 4 years old and your Aunt Phyllis was holding you as she cooked dinner." She looked away from me for a second. "Phyllis was always so kind to me. She snuck around letting me see you and play with you. When her husband found out she caught hell. I mean he beat her badly."

I held up my hand to stop her. I had never saw Uncle Pres raise his hand to anybody especially not Aunt Phyllis so I was didn't want to hear the rest of that story. "I would not tell you these things if they weren't true. Your father found out and threatened to never let them see you again and as you can imagine that killed her since she never had her own children. I was devastated when they died in that fire because they were very good to you. Eventually I got to speak to Dorian on the phone and he told me that I could see you if he was present. I was fine with that and sent for you both to come to New, York. You stayed in my condo and slept in the bed between us. I didn't have any unrealistic expectations about what we were going to do but he seemed to. He thought he could just ease back into my life but I was being selfish at the time because I was traveling so much for my job. I wanted to take you with me because he stayed deployed so much but he refused it and since I had no legal rights to you I had no argument."

I was starting to wonder is she would ever get to the point. I didn't need all of this history. The shit happened so long ago that it no longer mattered for real. I wondered if she really thought any of this would change what had happened. I still grew up to become a fairly decent man without her help so I didn't need her now. "The whole point is that me and Dorian spent years trying to make our relationship work for your sake. It was much easier to date here because interracial dating is so much more accepted than in my country. There were times he would stay on location with me for up to a month while your aunt and uncle had you. He would tell them he was being deployed and they took on the task of taking you in no questions asked."

Damn so pops was a liar too. This shit gets better and better. "So I guess instead of just hating you I am supposed to hate him too? You know what, hate is such a strong word. I will say that I dislike the way you carried things. I wish I had been able to have both of yall. I feel like you came in here with all your money trying to save the day." She looked up at the ceiling clasping her hands together. "You had all of the money you ever needed to be successful at least that's what I thought. When Dorian called me asking me for money to help you of course I said yes but I wondered what happened to the half a mil my father left you."

Did she really just say half a mil like it was five dollars? "Hold up," I said scooting up in the bed. "What's the deal with this money situation because all I knew about was what Uncle Pres and Aunt Phyllis left me?" She ran her hands through her mane. "I didn't want to go into all of this until you had a chance to speak to him first. When my father passed it was very hard. After I decided to give birth to you he somewhat disowned me. I was sent to relatives in Naples that weren't very nice to me. They had me working from sun up to sundown in their vineyards never caring about my condition. I was alienated from my own family so I hated him for that. To rid his conscience he left you that money and I stupidly out it into an account thinking your father would do right by it."

"So what did he do with it? He never mentioned it to me. I did everything I could do with the money my aunt and uncle left and he never asked me for a dime. I guess the nigga had so much fun spending my bread that he figured he may as well leave the second inheritance to me." My blood was boiling now. I couldn't wait to confront this nigga. "I am only telling you this because I think you need to know that money was never a factor in me coming to help you. I felt like I was finally going to be able to be in your life even if it was during a bad situation."

"All this time I been worried about how I would buy myself out of this trouble and this nigga sittin on stacks?" She furrowed her brows. "I don't think he is sitting on anything. The account was drained long ago so I don't know if he has any of it left. I do know that he did the best that he could take care of you which deserves some form of appreciation." I rubbed my eye which had started to twitch. Not only had she just told me pops had lied to me my whole life and had been fuckin around with her but now she was telling me that he had spent my inheritance but I should be thankful. I could feel myself about to blast her but the door opened. Just the nigga I needed to see....pops.

Chapter 32

Marissa

I was annoyed as I wrote down on the legal pad. I was tired and hurting. Thankfully the few burns I sustained were only 2nd degree but my hands and wrists where sprained from being thrown out of the house. The doctor said I was lucky the grass was so high because I surely would have broken something. As soon as my family left they brought these detectives in here asking me questions. I still couldn't speak so they came up with the bright idea of making me write down everything. I tried to recount everything as best as I could but I had been deprived of oxygen for a while making my memory sketchy. I could remember being in my car and going to Veronica's but I was so drunk at the times that I couldn't recall anything past that. As a matter of fact I was beyond drunk to the extent I felt like I had been slipped something. I wrote all of that down.

Detective Monroe as he identified himself did not look pleased at my statement. He looked up from the paper every few sentences to squint at me like he thought I was lying. He reminded me so much of Dewayne Johnson as he stood there with his Samoan features. His long hair was curly and very similar in texture to Delano's. "So this is all you can remember sweetheart?" I nodded my head yes. "Okay well get some rest I left my card in your side table if you need me okay?" I nodded again before he left the room speaking to who I guess was another detective. She looked back in at me giving me a pity smile before they walked down the hall. I was so relieved finally be left alone.

Because I couldn't talk it was gonna be difficult being in here. I couldn't even call my friends. Speaking of which I didn't even know if Veronica had made it out of the house. I wish I had thought to ask the detective about her. I was getting sleepy but I knew I would have to try to remember to ask about her. After the nurse came in to check on my blood pressure she gave me something for pain. The doctor came in shortly afterwards telling me that he was waiting on the results of my lab work. A few painful coughs produced a black substance that tasted like tar. Both of my sides were so I resorted to simply lying on my back to get relief. Eventually I drifted off to sleep never hearing my door creak open.

Shrouded in darkness I yanked on the chains to free myself. This must be what hell felt like. I could not see anything but the streetlight streaming through the tiny basement window. My lungs felt like I had drank a glass of liquid plumber with an ammonia chaser. Every time I tried to scream I couldn't get a sound to come out. My eyes and nose were both running as I rocked back and forth trying to chip the chair over. It dawned on me that if I hit the concrete floor the wrong way I would bust my head wide open. I was running out of options. As the smoke got thicker it felt like someone was choking me with their bare hands.

I can't believe she did this to me was all I could think. Moments of my best memories with Mona flashed by like the time we went to Kentucky Kingdom. I had two funnel cakes before getting on the rollercoaster Chang. Mama had warned me not to get on but as soon as she turned her back me and Mona used our VIP passes to skip to the front of the line. I threw up all over the place. Mama was mad as hell but daddy thought it was funny. Mona used her own money to buy me a t-shirt so that we didn't have to go home early.

Then there was the time when I first came on my period at school. I was in the fifth grade. I'll never forget it was picture day and you couldn't tell me nothing in my all white Levi jeans and matching jacket. When I stood up to get in the line my teacher pulled me to the side. She told me what happened and I was mortified. Taking the walk of shame to the office with a garbage bag tied around my waist I made the call to mama. She fussed about having to leave work early but she came and got me. She let me sit in the car on the bag of course, as she got me some pads. We stopped by Dairy Queen on the way home getting blizzards. I was so embarrassed to tell Mona but she assured me it was okay and told me how to put on my pad.

Most of my good memories involved Mona. She was always sure to make me feel better about myself no matter what the situation was. She didn't deserve how I had treated her at all. When I got to Atlanta and met Veronica she was so different than what I was used to. She was dancing in various clubs because she looked old enough. He brother had tatted her body up for her and she was having sex with whoever, whenever, wherever. Mona started becoming boring to me because all she was focused on was school. I wanted to hang out and have boyfriends but she was either into her books or into Todd.

He was sexy chocolate not doubt but I hated the way he treated her. She tried to play it off but I know she was not happy with him. She didn't know how to light em up and blow em out like candles the way I did. Going to the studio she used to feel so important until she saw he was bringing his other hoes there too. Plus Layla's clingy ass was always around the way. I had to set her straight once but she got the picture real quick. When I first laid down with Todd it was supposed to be a temporary thing. I never thought I would catch feelings. I certainly never thought I would be the side chick to the side chick.

It all became so clear now. I used to see Symphony in the studio but she always rocked the long weaves like Veronica. By the time me I was formally introduced to her she had her hair short and natural. I didn't recognize her at the time but she knew exactly who I was even though she never let on to the fact. I was in the dark but she had the light shining on me the whole time. I was about to pay for all my sins with my life.

The sound of a machine beeping brought me back to my present state. I opened my eyes looking into the face of pure evil. I could not even scream. The sound of the machine filled the entire room as the door flew open. I couldn't see anything but the back of a wheelchair as my door slammed shut. A nurse ran in flicking on the light. "Oh my goodness I was afraid something bad had happened it's just your IV twisted up." She assured me fixing it. Then she gave me an odd look. "Did you do this hun?" I didn't know what she was referring too. She held up a blue clamp. I shook my head no because I didn't understand. "Has someone been in here?" I shook my head yes. "Oh my goodness, hold tight dear I'll be right back. She disappeared for what seemed to be a quick second coming back with my doctor. "I think we have a problem because someone just put this clamp on her IV. Whoever it was knew that it would create an oxygen bubble which makes me believe they were trying to create a blood clot.

Chapter 33

Symphony

As soon as I got to the end of the hall I jumped out of the chair. My short hair was gonna pay off today because I looked like a straight up nigga from behind. I hoped I had enough time to kill that bitch before making my exit. As soon as the elevator opened I jumped in. I saw a nurse running towards me to catch the elevator but I let the doors slam in my face just in case she was about to try to be a hero. I ripped of the hospital gown balling it up. I had just enough time to throw it in the corner before the doors popped open. My nerves were shot as I rounded the corner. Veronica was double-parked waiting on me so I tried my best to walk fast without looking suspect. Thanks to Todd I had access to the hospital as well as a gown and wheelchair. I had done all of the dirty work but it would be worth it to have him to myself.

As soon as I got to the front lobby I could hear something being announced over the intercom. I wasn't about to stick around to hear what they were talking about though. I made my way to the front of the hospital where she was supposed to be waiting but of course her ass was somewhere else. I knew I should have made her run in but she would have just fucked it up. Walking away from prying eyes and nosey ass people standing around I waited until I got near the street to call her. She didn't answer her phone. *Damn, damn, damn.* I was on my Esther Rolle shit because I just knew I was about to be caught up due to her stupidity. A siren caught me off guard. I damn took off down the block before I realized it was only an ambulance. My nerves were definitely fried. I tried to figure out who else I could call for a ride. All of my brothers were either at work or in the trap. They never bothered to answer phone calls that weren't about money. You would think the bastards would have called once they found out our house had burnt down. It was just like them to be selfish. As I lit up a Newport I tried dialing Veronica again. She didn't answer but as soon as I hung up Todd was calling.

"Aye bae where you at?" I looked around trying to think of a lie. "I'm on my way to the crib." "Oh okay. Did you see what they did with my wheelchair? The transport people were looking for it." I was so damn slick I had to laugh at myself. As soon as his nurse stepped in to bathe him I grabbed his wheelchair and a gown sitting them by the door. I kissed him bye and then put my plan in motion. Contrary to popular belief I worked in a hospital before so I knew how to be slick with my shit. "Nope I didn't see it when I left." He paused for a second. "Oh okay. One of these lazy ass nurses probably grabbed my shift for their patient. Anyway, when you gonna come back up here and give me some head?" I wrinkled my nose in disgust hoping nobody was in the room with him. "I will probably see you tomorrow but look I gotta go this is my sister calling me." I lied getting him off the phone. I didn't even wait for a reply as I clicked over to my other call. "What's up, who is this?"

"This is Delano. I was trying to see if you wanted to listen to these beats I got in today." I looked at the weird number again. "Whose phone are you calling me from?" He laughed, "My phone came up missing last night I looked everywhere but I think some nigga from the studio got my ass." *That's what you get.* I thought to myself. "Nah I don't have time to even be thinking about music right now." I confessed dropping my cigarette onto the ground. I was really starting to think Veronica's ass had played me. "Okay I just thought I would give you the first choice since you are my first female artist. I guess I'll let Aria look over them." I couldn't stand the bitch Aria and would rather eat shoe leather than have her take a track from me. "Just hold onto it I will be by later." "Cool, I'll see you later." As soon as we disconnected the call I called Veronica back. She answered back this time. "Bitch where the fuck are you at?"

My mind was drawing a blank as to what to say. Delano's mother had

hit me with so much information in such a short time. This was definitely

out of control. I could not believe his daddy had been hiding the fact that

they had messed around for all these years. He deserved do much better

than that. The shouting match that took place when Mr. Dawson walked

into the room was one for the books. I kept hearing something about money

but Ms. Connie as she told me to call her, took me away from the scene.

"Bella do you think I did the wrong thing?" *I don't know who this*

Bella person was but it was annoying that she didn't remember my name.

"Ms. Connie I think it was bad timing for you to tell him but he deserved to

know the truth. Why do you keep calling me that though?" She laughed

speaking something in her language. The man in the passenger side seat

who had not said a word in front of me finally spoke in a thick accent. "Bella

means beautiful in Italian ma'am." I had to start blushing because I felt

silly. This was all too much for me to take in. I needed a drink and a bed in

that order. Pulling up to Delano's house I reached for the door handle to get

out. Ms. Connie slapped my hand lightly. "You never do what a man is

supposed to do Bella."

The man from the passenger side opened my door helping me out of the truck. "Keep in touch with me as I will be in town for a while." She said handing me a business card. I tucked it into my bra as she tossed me my car keys from the seat. "Be very careful." She remarked before he closed her door. They waited for my car to pull off. I was very leery about them driving behind me. I didn't know they were going to tail me all the way home. I had a feeling she knew more than she let on to me because in a few hours she had been more protective over me than my own mother had.

I turned on the radio to find them playing the same thing. Rap was the last thing I wanted to hear right now so I kept scanning through channels until I found one playing Sam Cooke. I loved having Sirius radio because they had something for everybody. I sung along to *Cupid* as I made my way home. I noticed that the driver was very careful to not let any cars get between us. He must have been used to this type of stuff. I sing along with the song thinking about Delano and how mush our lives had changed in such a short time. It seemed surreal that my ex, sister, and boyfriend where all in the hospital at the same time.

A little pang of guilt consumed me for not going to see Todd but after everything with him and Delano I just felt it wasn't a good idea. I had no idea what was going on with that since he didn't like to talk about it. I didn't like bring it up other to be honest. As I finally pulled up to my house the Navigator stopped at the edge of the driveway. Daddy opened the front door when he saw me. "Where the hell have you been Mona? We been calling you." I didn't want to tell him what all was going on so I just settled on the condensed version of the truth. "I went to see Delano." He frowned slightly. "Who is that woman?" I looked over my shoulder to see Ms. Connie walking up to us. *This is about to be very interesting.* "Hello sir my name is Constantina Giangula. I am Delano's mother." Daddy just stared at her outstretched hand and turning around I saw why. Just that quick her henchmen were standing behind her.

She turned around whispering something in Italian that pissed one of the men but a gesture she made with her hand caused him to throw his hands up in defeat. He retreated to the car while the driver stood there beside her. "As I was saying I am Delano's mother. May we speak inside please?" Not thinking he really had a choice daddy opened the door. I went to walk in with them but she gently grabbed my arms. "If you don't mind this is private Bella." I fell back somewhat relieved. I sat on the steps as the other man stared at me from where he was leaning on the truck. This was becoming team too much for me.

I walked back over to my car grabbing my phone. I saw that I had like 12 missed calls but most of them were from my parents. I wondered if mam had went to work. I couldn't tell if she was there because the garage door was closed. I saw a number I didn't recognize. It had called several times so I dialed it back. Ole dude was still staring as I sat back down on the front steps. I could hear laughter from inside the house which for me was a good sign. "Hello." The voice of an old lady had caught me off guard. She must have had the wrong number. "Hey, I saw this number on my caller ID and I was just calling back." There was a long pause. "Hello?" "I'm sorry baby I was watching my show let me see if my grandbaby called you. Veronica!!!!"

My heart went cold hearing that name. After what Delano told me I was not ever going to trust her snake ass again. We didn't know what role she played in this but she was definitely in cahoots with Veronica and Symphony. They were the last three to be with Marissa before everything went down. "Mona I am so glad I finally got you on the phone. Where are you at?" Not wanting to give her too much ammunition to meddle I casually replied, "I'm out and about." "Why you sound like you got an attitude?" She enquired.

"Why wouldn't I have an attitude when my sister almost got killed last night?" There was silence. "Oh my goodness Mona are you serious? I tried calling you but I could not find my phone for the life of me. All I know is I turned my back for a few minutes. The police were everywhere so I ran when everybody else ran. I got in the car and was like damn I can't even tell her what's goin on because her phone is in here. I went by the club yall weren't there so I went home. I figured you would call me from his phone."

Her story almost sounded believable except I did call her from Delano's phone and she kept sending it to voicemail. This bitch was obviously lying. "So you didn't see where my sister went?" "Girl when I looked up the police had cleared everybody out. Some other shit had popped off after yall left so they made everybody leave Mona. I swear I have no reason to lie to you. Delano showed up at my door with an attitude talking about give him your stuff.

"Leslie let's stop playing games because I know you are lying. Why the fuck would you have directions to Veronica's house in your phone?" "Huh? I don't even know that girl like that. I just know that she is Symphony's sister and I just found that out last night. I ain't never been to her house." I didn't even feel like talking to her. "Hold up? You got my phone? How did you get it?" "The same way you got her address Les! My sister almost burned up in that fuckin house!" "Mona what are you talking about I swear I.." I hung up inn her face. It was obvious she was in on this to begin with.

I cut my ringer off as Leslie called back. I knew she would try to come over here since she lived around the corner and when she did I would be ready for her ass.

"Thank you for clearing everything up for me. I know this is all craziness right now but we will have to have another sit down when you get the time." Daddy held the door open for her and the driver. I moved out of the way so they could get down the steps. "You are a prince of a man Jason. It was very nice meeting you and we will handle these matters as quickly as possible. I really hate these circumstances but your daughter is so beautiful and my son is lucky to have her."

"Aye what is luck when you are a Giangula?" Dad joked. Everyone laughed but me. I didn't find anything funny at the moment. When they got in the truck dad waved goodbye. As soon as they were out of our sight he snatched me inside the house locking the door. "What is wrong with you?" He rubbed his temples. "Mona have a seat. I sat down on the couch watching him pace. "Do you have any idea who those people are?" "All I know is that she used to model." He looked at me sideways. "She did way damn more than model Mona. She is part of the Giangula crime family."

I want surprised because I knew something was off about her swag but I also had never heard of them. "Daddy used to tell us stories about him when we were little. Those are some dangerous ass folks that I don't want to be affiliated with. She wants to do her own investigation into this whole fire incident. I say that my child is safe and her child is safe so we should let the police do their job but she wasn't trying to hear that. Now is one of those times I wish I had let you stay back home." "We had no way of knowing what was gonna happen daddy." He continued to pace, making me nervous. "Will you please sit down? You are gonna wear a hole through the floor." He scratched his chin thoughtfully. You don't fully understand what's going on right now. Not only does she want to solve this case but she also wants to know why your mother is living with her baby daddy.

I had forgot all about mama in the midst if everything else going on. This was about to be a mess of epic proportions. Not being able to take anything else I slowly ascended the stairs to my room when the doorbell rang. I was dead tired so daddy was just gonna have to get that himself. I was opened my bedroom door. "Mona! Leslie's at the door for you!" *So she decided to show her face after all.*

If I wasn't hemmed up in this hospital I would've choke slammed pops. He tried to come at me with excuses about how the hell he ran through half a million dollars that didn't even belong to him. I was mad as hell thinking back how he let me pay off our house when he had ran through my money. The worst part was knowing that he kept my mother away from me all this time. I was gonna need some time to get over that. I felt like I knew more about her than I did about him. I couldn't believe Uncle Pres had jumped on Aunt Phyllis about allowing my mother to see me. Mona was the only thing in my life that made sense and even that had become complicated with all the things that were going on now. It seemed like since I met her everything had started falling apart in my life.

I wondered if she was some type of bad luck or something. I truly loved her but we couldn't get along for shit. She was very childish and jealous which was highly unattractive to me and then her family was a whole different story. Mr. Middleton was cool I couldn't knock him but her mother and sister I couldn't really feel anything towards them. Although I had saved Marissa there was no doubt in my mind the way I felt about her snake ass. She was Mona's sister and that was the only damn reason I came looking for her. My instincts told me that Leslie was lying and my obligation to Mona made me look into the situation.

After talking to Symphony's dumb ass on the phone I was definitely sure she had a guilty conscience. I baited her to see if she would come down to the studio. I needed to see her face to face. Because I didn't have my wallet on me they weren't able to ID me at the scene so my name was never mentioned on the news coverage if she had seen it. I knew these muthafuckas was gonna try to keep me in here if nothing else but to let these detectives ask questions. I had to figure out an escape route so I could catch her when she came to the club. I still needed my phone though. I picked up the hospital phone hitting Cash. He was my last hope to getting this resolved. "Aye Cash where you at?" "Fam I been blowin up your phone all morning. Where you been at?" This was a long ass story that I wasn't trying to really relay to him right now. I knew time was of the essence of I wanted to catch Symphony slippin.

"It's a long ass story but I'm in Grady Memorial." "SHADY GRADY? The hell you doin in there?" "It's a very long story trust me. I need you to come through though. It's some major shit goin down that we gotta take care of like yesterday." "I am on my way bruh, sit tight." After disconnecting the call I realized I didn't even know what room number I was in. I was about to call for a nurse when a flashing news bulletin caught my attention. It was showing coverage of the house fire. Turning up the volume I was able to catch the last few seconds of what they were saying. My head hit the pillow hard as hell as I realized that I had made a careless mistake.

This shit would make the newspapers because only the dumbest of criminals forgets their gun at a crime scene. The same gun that I had shot Todd with was about to be tagged and bagged as evidence. I was official chopped and screwed. There was no way this shit could get any worse than it was right now. My arms started throbbing so I went ahead and called my nurse. "Mr. Dawson what's the matter?" She even tried to sound flirty on the nurse call button. I had to chuckle a little bit because she was staring me down earlier. She had even washed my hair to remove any shards of glass left in. "My arm is hurting real bad can I get something for pain now?"

"I will be right there." She replied. After a few minutes she came in carrying a pill that looked like it was too big for a horse to swallow. "Uh what the hell am I gonna do with that?" "I can break it in half for you but it really is important you take the whole thing." I always hated medicine as a child and this was no exception. "Just open your mouth and I will put it in for you." Something about the way she said that seemed sexual but I let it go. I gulped down the pill will damn near half a can of sprite. "Do you need anything else?" I couldn't think of anything so I said no.

"Let me make sure your IV is good." Instead of walking around the bed she leaned over me. Her titties were resting on my face as she adjusted it. If I didn't get out of her soon Mona would swear something was going on. Speaking of which I wondered how she was doing. As soon as Nurse flirty left I called Mona. "Hello." She answered after the third ring. "Hey ma how you feelin?" "I am dead tired." She replied yawning. "Can you believe Leslie came over here trying to me? She said something about she didn't see Marissa's car pulling off but I knew she was lying because how did Cash see it?" Now that she put the question in my head I thought about it too. Where was Cash at that he could see everything and she didn't? I would be sure to ask him that and I wouldn't have to wait long because he walked into my roomed flanked by two police officers. *Ain't this a female dog?"*

Chapter 36

Marissa

They had asked me a million times but my answer remained the same. All I saw was the back of the head. It was a dark-skinned guy with a very low fade that had come into my room. I was alarmed when I realized I was in the same hospital as Todd. I was completely out of it when they brought me in or else I would asked them to take me somewhere else. There was no way I wanted to be anywhere near them. An officer was stationed at my door now which made me feel a little bit safer as I waited on my parents to arrive. Mama was such a nervous wreck she decided to leave work early.

I hoped her and daddy acted as loving as they did earlier because Lord knows the last thing I wanted to hear was arguing. I had enough of that from them two to last a lifetime. The doctor promised me that they would review the camera's to see if they could find the person that had snuck into my room but I was sure it was Todd. He must have gotten wind of everything going on by now but I wondered if he was well enough to be wheeling himself around. The person in that wheelchair was moving pretty quickly. When I saw mama's face peer around my door I lit up.

"I wanted to be careful not to wake you but I see you are already up."

She padded into the room looking like she worked here in her hospital

scrubs. Sitting her work bag down on the chair she hugged me kissing my

forehead. A knock at the door grabbed both of our attention. "Who is it?"

mama asked. "It's her father." The officer stationed at my door answered.

"He can come in." Mama replied. We were both in a word of surprise as a

very sexy, tall chocolate man with curly hair appeared carrying flowers." He

looked at mama then at me smiling. "I think I may be here at the worst

possible time but I am here." I looked up at mama who seemed to be

transfixed on him. I tapped her arm. Slowly her eyes made contact with

mine. Here was Mr. Ivory Cooke in the flesh. My world was officially

thrown off balance. What happened next? That's another story.

Made in the USA
Monee, IL
14 January 2021